Dead End

Tales

Murderous Mayhem

and

Spooky Spectres

The Whittlesey Wordsmiths

Disclaimer

Fictional tales in this collection are inventions of the writer, including their characters.

Unless otherwise stated, any resemblance to any person, living or dead, is coincidental, whatever our relatives might claim.

Murderous Mayhem and Spooky Spectres

The ladies of Whittlesey Wordsmiths are rarely short of ideas for killing off their husbands, while our gentlemen tend to seek further afield for their virtual victims (fearing, perhaps, to upset their wives.)

Some of the slain would like to get their own back.

Others just want to be heard.

CONTENTS

Dead End Tales

Dead End Tales

Dead End Tales

Dead End Tales

Now Just Think About What You Have Done

Wendy Fletcher

Alice caught her breath. She had been about to say those very words to three-year-old Lyra as she placed her firmly on the naughty step.

Instead, it was Lyra's voice, yet not Lyra's normal voice.

She pinned her mother to the spot with a cold, narrow-eyed stare and the deep bass tone seemed to be generated from low down in her tiny body. She held the stare until Alice was forced to look away.

When Lyra's father, Scott, got home that night, Alice recounted the happenings of the day, but she didn't mention the incident on the step at the foot of the stairs. Only much later, when Lyra was tucked up after a bath and a bedtime story, did he notice his wife's quiet mood and ask, 'You OK?'

'Yeah. I think so.'

'You don't sound too sure. Let's pour a glass of wine. Then you can tell me what's bothering you.'

'It probably sounds silly.' Alice clutched the stem of her glass. 'It was just something Lyra said earlier. It spooked me a bit.'

She told him how Lyra pre-empted the words she was going to say to her, but Scott just laughed and said that obviously she had heard it all before and was getting in there first.

Alice did remember saying it before, so she couldn't argue about that, but she felt Scott was missing the bigger point. He wasn't there. He hadn't seen the accusing stare or heard the depth of that voice.

'It was almost...' she tried again. 'Almost... menacing.'

'Oh, come on, Alice. She's three.'

'I said you would think I was being silly.'

She left it there, seeing no point in trying to describe something she couldn't understand herself.

The next day passed without incident. In fact, the whole week was quite unremarkable. Then on Friday, she caught Lyra throwing a hard plastic brick at the TV screen.

'Off again to the naughty step.' She sighed when Lyra threw it again despite a warning and laughed in her face.

'You're not funny.'

Alice stepped back. That was it again. The very words she was about to use. The look. The voice.

'It happened again today.'

Scott was hardly in the door this time before she blurted it out.

'Alice, she's a small child, mimicking what she hears. Don't make it sound so sinister.'

'Well, it's weekend now, so I just hope she does it while you're home.'

'Yes, so do I. Then we can laugh at her together. It sounds like she's becoming quite the little actress, and I don't want you stressing. It's not good for this one.'

He ran a gentle hand over the growing bulge they already knew from the scan was going to be Lyra's little brother.

Of course, nothing happened over the weekend while Scott was home, but Monday morning, not twenty minutes after he left for work, Alice found Lyra rifling through the make-up in her bedroom drawer.

'You are not supposed to be in here. Get out now.'

This time the words were strung together into a sentence longer than Lyra had ever said before and her eyes were so tightly squeezed together that Alice could no longer see the colour of them.

Without replying to the child, she turned away, left her to her rummaging, and went downstairs to phone Scott.

'Darling, I can't drop everything and come home.' His was the voice of reason.

'Well, you're going to have to. I can't do this anymore.' Hers was the high-pitched squeal of panic.

'OK, I'll be there in fifteen minutes, but then we are going to see Dr Carmichael. I think you need something to calm you down.'

'Yes, whatever. Just get home.'

Alice put the phone down before he could change his mind, but she didn't go back upstairs. Instead, she sat in the kitchen watching the door that led into the hall until she heard the car pull in.

'Daddy's home. Daddy's home.'

Lyra ran down and greeted Scott with her sweet lisping voice and a wide-eyed smile.

He scooped her into his arms and nuzzled her neck, but over her shoulder his look for Alice was less kind.

'Come on. Let's get this sorted. I don't know if it's your hormones or stress levels or what. Hopefully the doctor will work it out 'cus I'm sure I can't. It's almost like you're afraid of Lyra.'

Alice followed them out, thinking, 'I think I am. I'm going crazy. Being freaked out by a three-year-old. How am I going to manage with a new baby too?'

She had to agree that the doctor was as helpful as he could be. He didn't think she should take any medication at this late stage of the pregnancy, assured her that an occasional glass of wine was unlikely to do any harm, but made the best suggestion of all right at the end.

'Couldn't Scott start his paternity leave a little earlier?'

Of course, he could. He was his own boss. He only needed to arrange cover for the office. Alice was so relieved. Lyra was a different child when Scott was at home. Well, actually she was her normal child-self. She played and was still mischievous, but never outrageous. She chatted in a three-year-old way – never in long sentences – and they could enjoy bonding before the newbie arrived.

It was a plan that worked well. The birth went smoothly. Little Finn was a good weight and allowed home late the same day. Alice was feeling much less stressed now they had spent those last three weeks as a family unit.

By the time the day came for Scott to start back to work, she was feeling much more confident. There had been no more scary moments with Lyra. Perhaps it had all been a game. Now she was too busy to play it anymore as she fetched nappies and carried bottles, doting on her new little brother.

'Mum's coming over at lunch time to make sure I'm OK. You know how she worries.' She called out to Scott as he got into the car. 'I might take the tinies and walk down to meet her at the bus station.'

'Good idea.' Scott called back. 'Do you good to get some exercise.'

Alice laughed. Scott had been teasing her about the extra pounds suiting her, but she knew he was relieved to know that she was eating properly again, they could laugh together. Life felt good.

She stepped back inside, and the voice met her.

'Now just think about what you have done.'

She didn't need to look in the silent cot.

Death by Parrot

Jane Pobgee

In 1929, Maria was given her bird by her father when she was twelve years old. It was a rare Hyacinth Macaw (a blue parrot). Growing up, she took great care of it, named him Percy and he became very tame with her but didn't like being handled by anyone else.

As Maria grew up, she taught Percy to speak. Not only did he have a wide vocabulary, he was also a great mimic.

Maria grew to womanhood and eventually found herself a soulmate. To make everything perfect, his name was Philip Parrot, so on her wedding day she became Mrs Parrot. They moved to a small first-floor flat not far from her parents. Everything was as she imagined married life would be and, of course, Percy came too.

Philip liked Percy, but Percy did not like Philip, and when he came home from work Maria needed to make sure Percy was in his cage so he would not attack Philip. Over time Philip began to dislike Percy and the bird's close relationship with his wife. He was jealous.

Their marriage was not blessed with offspring and although they were sad about this, they continued with their lives, enjoying being able to go out or on holiday whenever they wished. Maria's dad would always babysit Percy.

As the years passed, Philip's dislike turned to hatred of Percy. He tried to get Maria to part with him, even going so far as to leave the windows open and opening Percy's cage. Unfortunately for him, Percy didn't fly off, but attacked Philip until he had to leave the room with claw marks on his head and arms. This was now causing arguments in their marriage, and they had many loud shouting matches about Percy, which their neighbours overheard.

They had been married over twenty years when it happened. Maria was home from work early and had allowed Percy out of his cage to be with her. Philip came in from work. Usually, Percy was back in his cage before this happened, but she had totally forgotten the time, and Percy was out and about.

Philip walked in, and Percy attacked him. Philip was furious. When Maria caught Percy and was taking him to his cage, Philip ran after her and pulled and clawed at her arms, trying to get to the bird. She screamed, "Philip, stop it, please," but in her urge to protect her bird, Maria lost her balance. She fell backwards, releasing Percy, but unable to stop herself falling. She landed with a sickening thud. Her head hit the marble hearth, and she died instantly.

Of course, their neighbours heard the scream and the thud, followed by silence. They phoned the police as they were concerned. Philip had rushed from the room as Percy started attacking him. He managed to close the door and telephoned for an ambulance.

The police arrived just before the ambulance and asked what had happened. Philip started to explain when Percy shrieked, "He did it, he did it, he did it!"

The paramedics could do nothing for Maria, and she was pronounced dead at the scene.

The police questioned the neighbour who made the emergency call and heard how the couple had many loud and vicious-sounding arguments. They took Philip away to be questioned, as they were not satisfied with his answers.

The postmortem found that Maria's death was caused by her head hitting the marble hearth, but they were suspicious of the scratches on her arms which looked like defence wounds. Philip told them the scratches were caused by the parrot, but they checked and found her skin under his fingernails. He explained he was trying to get the bird, but no one believed him.

Maria's Father offered to look after Percy. Every day the parrot would repeat, "He did it, Philip killed Maria." Maria's Father reported what the bird was saying to the police. He was sure Philip had hurt his wife and caused her death.

The evidence was very thin and mainly circumstantial, but in the end, Philip was charged with murder. After four days of deliberation, the jury found him guilty.

The death penalty was asked for and granted. Eventually Philip was hung from the neck until he died, innocent of everything except hating a parrot.

Death by parrot.

What Next?

Cathy Cade

Where am I now? One minute I'm floating above a hospital bed looking down at the rest of me, and then everything sort of dissolves and I'm here. I don't recall lying in a hospital bed. I recall being in the passenger seat of Adam's car on the cliff road.

I recall us hurtling too fast at a bend, through the blue-taped gap in the fence and out… gazing through the windscreen at grey-white clouds, and the weight of the car dropping through mid-air. I don't recall landing. I recall darkness and pain and voices before the pain dulled.

Mists fell and never lifted. Now the muzziness has cleared, but confusion remains. Is this the gateway to heaven or the road to hell? Where is the light I'm supposed to follow? Where is Adam? He was angry and driving too fast. Angry enough to misjudge that corner?

Adam rarely travelled on that road up to the convalescent home, where wealthy celebrities and tycoons enjoy the clear air, scenic views and seclusion, while recovering from their excesses. Did he intend to kill us both? Not the Adam I knew. However angry he might have been.

It's true, he had been different lately: phoning me at work; coming home during the day; jumping up to answer the phone as soon as it rang… I was beginning to wonder if he was having an affair. But that wouldn't have been my Adam, either.

He had been furious when he read Craig's stupid note, but still, when my car wouldn't start and I was late for my shift, he offered me a lift to work. That was my Adam. What was Craig thinking? Leaving that stuck through the letterbox?

He'd addressed it to *Darling Jules* and offered, in a suggestive tone, to be my chauffeur whenever I needed one. It had been signed, *Forever Yours*, with kisses. Not even in an envelope. He must have thought I'd find it on my way out.

I suppose he didn't realise that Adam might come home during the day. And thinking of home, I found myself there, in our living room where Adam accused me this morning: "I knew it! You're having an affair with that arrogant b–."

"Don't be ridiculous. That's just his way. You know Craig." Craig always expressed himself extravagantly in life, as on screen. We'd got on well when he was recovering from a bit of a breakdown after his ex went off with a footballer.

He keeps an apartment nearby where he spends a lot of time between TV appearances. "I think he's lonely, Adam. He doesn't know many people locally. It doesn't mean anything." He had almost adopted us since he left the convalescent home.

I enjoyed Craig's elaborate turn of phrase and wicked sense of humour. Adam said he had a spiteful streak. "I saw him dropping you off in that flashy sports car last week. You said you were out with 'the girls'."

I'd shrugged. "He just turned up. It saved me a cab fare. Anyway, Craig almost is one of the girls." My giggle had angered Adam. He thought I was laughing at him. I should have taken him more seriously.

His face reddened. "Don't think I haven't seen the way he looks at you when he thinks I'm not watching. Like a cat watching a mouse, deciding when to pounce." This low growl wasn't the Adam I knew.

"He was lurking out there this morning when I went out to the car. His car must have been parked out of sight somewhere, which is a giveaway in itself. Waiting for me to leave, was he?"

He'd stormed out before I could think of a response. I'm sure Adam must have mistaken someone else for Craig. But still, when my car wouldn't start, he offered to drive me to work, bless him.

And now, here he was, as if I'd conjured him up by thought alone. I sensed rather than saw him until my thoughts gave him form. I felt his reproach before he gave it words.

"How could you think that of me?" It took me a moment to tune in to what he meant, so he repeated it. "How could you believe I would drive us over a cliff?"

"How could you believe I'd be unfaithful with Craig?" But I realised that he no longer believed I would; just as I now understood that he hadn't deliberately driven us off the road.

The doorbell rang. Craig was outside as if summoned by us – only in the flesh. Unlike us. Now he hammered on the door. "Jules, please be there. Please come to the door."

He moved to the window and peered in. But, of course, he didn't see us. He banged on the window, anyway. "Jules, please, please be here. Tell me it isn't true."

Most of the neighbours will have been at work, but across the road a curtain twitched, and a passing schoolgirl hesitated before speeding up across our driveway and hurrying on.

Craig returned to the doorbell and pressed it several times before banging again, but eventually he gave up, collapsing onto the doorstep like an inflatable doll with a puncture.

Between sobs, he was mumbling something I couldn't make out at first. After a while, though, it became easier to understand: he was so sorry, he hadn't meant...

And then he'd break into fresh sobs, punctuated by hiccups. Occasionally a large sob erupted, and he'd groan, "I love you, Jules," or "I'll always love you."

I sensed an element of grim triumph in Adam's reaction to Craig's distress. He had been right in his assessment of Craig's feelings, if not mine.

Not that it mattered now. We appeared to understand each other's feelings perfectly. It seemed a shame we hadn't been so intuitive while still alive.

"Poor Craig. But it was his fault that you were so angry with him – with us. So, it's partly his fault that we're dead."

"You mean that otherwise I wouldn't have been driving the car so fast into that bend. But that wasn't what happened at all."

He must have sensed my puzzlement. "I wasn't driving fast. It was the incline that caused us to speed. The brakes failed."

That made no sense. Adam's car was serviced only last week and passed its MOT test. The brakes were fine then.

A neighbour – she of the twitching curtains – must have called the police. They turned up and spoke gently to him.

They asked what the matter was, which resulted in fresh tears and incoherent explanations. They encouraged him to stand.

When he quickly collapsed again on the doorstep, they realised that he wouldn't leave of his own will.

We watched, not attempting to leave the house. Somehow we knew; we were meant to be here.

We wouldn't be able to leave our home – not yet. We were here for a reason.

The police had persuaded Craig he should go with them to receive help and counselling.

He stood and, between his sobs, they heard, "Jules wasn't meant to be there."

The officers looked at each other. Their brows lifted and their backs straightened.

Their movements became more purposeful as they led him to their car.

The policewoman went around the other side to sit beside him.

The policeman held the door open as he got in.

Then, the policeman started to close the car door.

Craig turned back to look at the house.

His eyes widened, as if seeing us.

He looked straight into my eyes.
I'll swear he saw me.
He cried out again.
One final farewell.
A howl.
"Jules!"

~ ~ ~

Ever-decreasing paragraphs.

This is one of several ghost stories (and a memoir) in this collection that were written to the additional challenge of a wordcount limit.

Beginning with a paragraph of 50 words, the next paragraph has 49 words, then 48… down to a final single-word paragraph.

How long did it take you to realise something was up?

Look out for more…

Angel

Philip Cumberland

An old white Transit van pulled up at the level crossing but on the wrong side of the road.

It was early on a May morning; the sun had not long risen and wasn't fully about its business. The road ran through an isolated part of the fen. Even later in the day, few vehicles used it, which was why Wilf had chosen it.

The crossing light turned amber. The two above it flashed red, the warning buzzer started to sound, and the barriers descended. The engine was running; with his foot on the clutch, he put the van into gear.

Then nothing happened.

Before he could release the clutch, his father, who died ten years earlier, was sitting beside him, knocking the van out of gear and pulling up the handbrake.

His father looked through the windscreen and said, "You can go now, lads. I have him."

Six firemen stood up, appearing in the windscreen. They had been pushing against the front of the van to hold it from moving.

Dad had been a fireman, and Wilf recognised some of the faces as his mates.

One turned and said, "Okay. If you're sure."

"Thanks, Pete. It's okay now. Thanks, all of you."

With that, they disappeared.

"Turn the engine off, Wilf, and come with me."

Wilf switched off the engine, opened the door, and climbed out of the van, but as his feet touched the ground they were smaller.

So was he.

His father, now younger and taller than him, had walked around the van and took Wilf's small hand in his, leading him towards a field gate.

As they approached the gate, the field beyond changed into the common Wilf had played on when he was younger. A few of his friends were there too, running around shrieking and laughing.

Dad led him over to his mum, younger too now. Beside her lay the dogs that his parents and he had owned. One by one, they raced up to him, tails wagging. They stood on their hind legs to lick him and rolled on their backs to have their tummies tickled.

The small girl sitting next to his mother intrigued Wilf, until he realised he was looking at his Aunt Janet, who died aged three, long before he was born. He had seen the one photo his mum had of her sitting on a blanket on the floor.

It dawned on him that everyone he was seeing around him had died. He went over to his mother and put his arms around her.

"This is your Aunt Janet, Wilf. Say hello."

"Hello, Aunt Janet."

"Hello, Wilf. Your mum has told me so much about you."

Wilf's dad came back to collect him, then introduced him to relatives and ancestors, some of whose names he had heard but by no means all. Every one of them was pleased to see him.

"Time to take you back, Wilf. It's not yet the time for you to join us."

"But how, Dad; why?"

"Within you are bits of every one of your ancestors, as they are in me and all these people, your family, you see here. There is a poem by William Blake, called *Auguries of Innocence*, and one line in it gets close to things: 'To see the world in a grain of sand.' All these bits of us are in you. They are in something so small you would only see the thing containing it with a powerful microscope, and you wouldn't see what's inside even then."

Wilf found himself back beside the van, taller now, back to the age he had been in the van.

His father let go of his hand, hugged him, and stood back to look at him.

"Your problems will go away, Wilf. We are watching you and helping you. When it is time for you to join us, I will come for you, but don't try to get here earlier. You carry us all with you; look after us too. Cheerio, son."

With that, he was gone.

Wilf climbed back in the van, made sure there were no trains coming, and drove off carefully.

He now knew he had a lot of people to look after.

The House on the Hill

Valerie Fish

People say that the place is haunted,
The house at the top of the lane.
It's said that folk who venture there
Never come back down again.

The tale goes that the master took an axe
To his wife and children, one by one.
Then, with a pistol, blew out his brains
When he realised what he'd done

And, although long dead and buried,
Their restless spirits still remain,
And ghostly cries can oft be heard
A long way down that spooky lane.

Mother always told us girls,
'Don't ever go up that hill.'
But we thought it all one big scream,
And we were up for a thrill,

Dead End Tales

What happened that night I cannot tell.
The things I saw and heard
Will haunt me till my dying day,
But I'll never breathe a word.

Sometimes I wish it wasn't me
That came back down that lane,
But instead, my baby sister
Who was never seen again.

Jane Pobgee

A Murder

Stephen Oliver

Sometimes, you can get away with murder because no one will ever suspect you.

I flew in as soon as I heard about it. Fortunately, I wasn't too far away, so it was a short trip.

When I arrived, the body was still on the ground, surrounded by curious figures. I strode up, shoving some of the rubberneckers out of the way.

They'd just turned the body over as I approached, and I felt a surge of emotion pour over me, stopping me dead in my tracks for a moment.

It was my eldest son, Zeke.

"How did this happen?" I asked Joshua, Zeke's younger brother, who stood on the other side of the body, staring at me with his beady eyes. "Who did this?"

"We don't know how it occurred," he replied, his voice croaking with emotion. "He was out here on his own, scouting around. However, word has it that Ephraim Giles was spotted walking away from this field, carrying a shotgun." Somehow, I wasn't surprised. Giles has hated us and our kind for years.

After all, this land has been ours by ancestral birthright since long before Giles and his ilk turned up to mark it out, fence it off, and take possession of it. And many of them hate us because they know they've stolen what's rightfully ours, so they pretend we're the bad guys. But we've been living off this land for centuries and millennia.

His personal hatred of us and our ways went so deep that I'd overheard him use racial slurs against us on a regular basis.

"Nasty little —— bastards," he'd shout as he chased after us. "Always coming on my land, stealin' and crappin' the place up."

The thing is, this wasn't even "his" field in the first place. It "belonged" to Silas Jones, his neighbour, a much more reasonable man who appreciated that we had as much right to be here as he did.

So, not only had Giles committed murder, but he'd also been trespassing.

I'd been staring down at the corpse for a while, looking at the bleeding holes in his body, when Joshua prodded me.

"What are we going to do now, Dad?"

The wash of grief turned almost instantly to rage.

"Can you start with... the proceedings?" I asked him. "I've got to do something first."

"Of course, Dad." I saw him nod to a couple of others to come and help him as I turned away.

Deciding not to go directly after Giles, I made my way to the woods nearby and began flitting from tree to tree, trying to remain concealed. Once the trees gave out, I used the hedgerow along the road as cover, approaching within a few yards of the farm's entrance.

At this point, it became a case of sneaking around the scattered farm equipment, hiding behind each, and scanning ahead to choose the next place to run to.

When I turned the corner to the back of the house, I spotted Giles nearby. I pulled back and stuck only the top of my head around the brickwork.

He appeared to be pottering around the small garden, selecting vegetables, probably for his evening meal. I could hear him muttering to himself in glee.

"Heh, heh, heh, got another of the little bastards, I did. Kill 'em all! None on my land if I can help it."

I froze as he turned toward me, but he was only putting a handful of potatoes on the table next to carrots, swedes, and parsnips. He didn't notice me peeking around the corner.

He continued his gleeful rant as he turned back and headed for the cabbage patch. I heard words like "eradicate", "annihilate", and "little —— bastards" float back over his shoulder as he bent.

Then I spotted it!

He'd leaned his shotgun against the table, apparently intending to head out to kill again while his supper cooked. I thought its position looked a little precarious as I sneaked closer to take a look.

It was a nasty-looking weapon, evidently well-used in killing my kin and others.

As Giles turned back to the table with a large cabbage in his hands, I shoved against the shotgun, causing it to topple over toward him.

I was in luck.

It appeared to have a hair-trigger because both barrels fired simultaneously as it slid along the table and landed on the arm of a chair, blasting shot at him at almost point-blank range.

I still remember the shock on his face as he saw it falling, aiming almost perfectly at him. His eyes widened as he spotted me next to the falling weapon.

Then the discharge wiped the surprise off his face, along with his features, as the pellets tore holes in him from hairline to sternum, leaving behind a bloody mess much worse than on my son's body.

He fell over backwards, and his corpse made a satisfying thump as it hit the ground.

I stood savouring the sensation of revenge as the body twitched and relaxed into death.

"Rest in peace, Zeke," I said as I turned away. "Your murder has been avenged."

As was my nature, I returned to the field directly, ready to join in the funerary rites with the rest of the clan. Their cries of woe and grief echoed around the countryside, informing all of Zeke's demise.

When I approached the field, I noticed Silas Jones and his grandson standing hand in hand by the hedge, staring at the throng in the centre of the field.

As I passed them, the boy turned to the old man.

"Grandad," Little Lewie asked, pointing at the crowd, "why do they call them a 'murder' of crows?"

Death in the Family

Rita P Skeats

"Eunice is gone! She's dead!" shrieked Zimbi as she entered the staff room.

I stared at her in disbelief. It was only a few days ago I had worked with Eunice, and she was well.

"What happened?" I managed to splutter.

"Died of a heart attack early this morning in A&E. Worked the night shift at King George and fell ill while on duty."

Zimbi buried her face in her hands and began to sob, overwhelmed by the news of Eunice's death. They were close friends and came from Southern Africa. They shared the same values. I allowed her to rest in the staff room for a while and over a cup of tea at break time, she disclosed further information about Eunice.

"Her husband was not a good man – very controlling and nasty. Made her work all hours God sent. And mother-in-law lived with her – a domineering woman. Eunice didn't have a life. She was chained to them, and worked like a slave. They killed her." She sobbed with fear in her dark eyes.

We attended Eunice's funeral. I had known her for over five years. She was very jovial and lively and seemed to be on a "high" all the time. She spoke of her life growing up in Zimbabwe; it evoked happy memories for her. She never spoke of her family life in the UK.

At the crematorium, Zimbi pointed out Eunice's husband to me. He was indeed a fearsome figure, tall and broad, with a permanent scowl. He barked at his four children to stay huddled in a corner of the room. Their expressions were of fear and loss. Next to him stood a tall, slim woman. Dressed in native African outfit, she was decked in yellow jewellery, and wore bright red lipstick. She curled her fingers into his hand.

"The new mother for the children." Zimbi gestured in her direction. "Not a good woman. They wanted Eunice out of the way." She tutted. "He killed her."

The coroner's report revealed that a large amount of stimulant drug was found in Eunice's body. It was concluded that she took the drugs regularly to enable her to work without becoming tired and it might have brought on the heart attack.

Zimbi was severely affected by Eunice's death and became withdrawn. I tried to find out about her family, but she would not disclose information. She was naturally a private person and quiet by nature. I gave her space but offered my assistance if needed.

Two months later, I heard that Zimbi was murdered. It was in the national newspapers splattered on the front pages: "Midwife murdered by husband." A quiet person she was. She did not invite attention. Ironically, her story was exposed for everyone to read.

Zimbi's husband murdered her by strangulation after she threatened to leave him. He was unfaithful and abusive to her for many years, but she persevered with the marriage because of her children.

A close friend had offered Zimbi accommodation, and she was on the verge of leaving the family home when the husband appeared. Soon after strangling her, he hanged himself. His domineering mother, who had lived with them, was not in the house at that time. The bodies were found by their children after they returned from school.

Six months later, Dr Farina Ali, another work colleague, was found dead at home. I had discharged her after she gave birth and there was nothing to suggest that she was not of sound mind. Staff in the maternity unit were shocked by her death. She was well liked by all her colleagues and patients.

Ms Hargreaves, the consultant obstetrician, knew Farina well and disclosed to staff that she was living with her husband and mother-in-law. She supposedly suffered from postnatal depression after her discharge from hospital and committed suicide five days later. It was rumoured that Farina suffered emotional and domestic abuse at the hands of her husband and mother-in-law, and she was made to commit suicide. After her funeral, the husband married his mistress.

I thought that the deaths of my colleagues followed a pattern: domestic and emotional abuse, domineering mothers-in-law, intensive workloads, and cultural problems. Although they were in positions to act as advocates for clients facing domestic abuse, they were not able to save themselves. They had lost their identity – an annihilation of oneself.

Dead End Tales

"Watch your husbands, girls." Ms Hargreaves chuckled. "You don't know who will be the next victim."

I have been watching mine ever since. I do not want to be bumped off in favour of the mistress.

Jane Pobgee

The Attic

Jane Pobgee

Laura was delighted when they moved in. They were young, vibrant people obviously in love. She loved hearing their laughter. The young woman would often sing to herself as she completed her daily chores around the house, rushing to greet and kiss her man as he came home from work.

She led him to his favourite armchair, fetching his slippers before laying the table for the meal she had cooked. Sharing their news about their days seemed so idyllic – such a change to how things were when Laura first lived here. Life for these two seemed tender and sweet.

Slowly, things began to change. He started to complain about how she cooked his meals, ironed his clothes, and kept house. She tried harder to please him but always fell short. Eventually, more and more arguments occurred, until one day he hit her. She could not believe it.

He was sorry, begged her for forgiveness and promised it would never ever happen again. But it always did. She no longer sang as she did her chores or ran to greet him. She approached with fear and trepidation in her eyes, which angered him even more.

Laura watched as the beautiful vibrant woman became a shadow of herself. She was constantly tired. She lost her joy and slowly became grey and silent. She moved slowly about the house, often in pain from the beatings she had received. Her sadness permeated the building.

As Laura watched this happen, she was screaming out to her, "Leave him, leave him before it's too late." But of course, the woman couldn't hear her or see her. Laura's ghost walked the floors of the house seeing everything but able to do nothing.

Laura was determined to help if she could, but how? She didn't want the woman to end up like her: another statistic of domestic violence, murdered by her abusive husband; her body hidden in the attic, never found; her husband getting away with murder.

She tried lots of ways of talking to this woman, who couldn't hear her. She tried to move objects to get her attention, but she couldn't do it. She exhausted herself trying a hundred different ways but just couldn't break through to her.

All the while, Laura was trying to reach the woman, things were getting steadily worse for her. The screaming and shouting, the bullying and the beatings seemed to be never ending. Her spirit was broken. She never fought back or defended herself.

Laura wondered how much more the poor woman could take? She felt certain that if she could not get through to her soon, then it would be only a matter of time before her broken body joined Laura's in the attic.

As Laura watched, she noticed that the young woman often tossed and turned during bad dreams at night and would wake the next day even more exhausted than before. She sometimes mumbled in her sleep. That gave Laura an idea.

Laura began to hover over her bed, and when she had a bad dream she would whisper in her ear to calm her. It seemed to work. Her subconscious responded to Laura, and her fears seemed to pass away.

Laura was jubilant. She had found a way to communicate at last. Slowly, she began to tell her story to the young woman about who she was, what had happened to her, and where her body lay hidden.

At first, she knew the woman was frightened and horrified that there could be a body in her attic. Over time she accepted what she thought she had dreamed and needed to see the evidence for herself.

Whilst her husband was out, she climbed to the attic. Directed by what she thought was instinct, she went straight to the far corner, searching for evidence. Eventually, by removing a wall panel, she found it.

The young woman thought she should call the police, and Laura said, "No!" forcefully. The woman reacted instantly, looking around and saying, "Who said that?" Laura spoke again, and the woman heard her whilst awake.

Laura told the woman she was trapped here, but she would be free when she had a proper burial. The woman wanted to get this done at once, but Laura asked her to wait.

Intrigued, the woman sat quietly on the floor as Laura explained that she wanted to help the woman and stop the same thing happening to her. The problem was, how to do it?

They couldn't think of a solution straight away, but the breakthrough had been made, and they could talk things over whenever they wanted now. They discussed many plans but most were unworkable.

The woman told Laura that her name was Penny. Her husband had told her if she tried to leave, he would kill her, and both of them believed that he would.

After much discussion, they came to the realisation that, for Penny to escape, meant her husband had to die. Accepting that fact was easier, as Penny no longer loved him.

A change came over Penny. She began to have hope that there was a way out of this. Unfortunately, this didn't go unnoticed. Her husband responded with his fists.

Battered and bruised, she was comforted by Laura, and they decided, whatever the plan, they could not wait much longer, as Penny may not survive the next onslaught.

They finally came up with a plan. Penny would lure him to the attic and Laura, using her new skills would push him and the ladder over.

With luck, the fall would kill him, and Penny would finally be safe. It was the best plan in the time they had left to them.

Every chance they had, Laura would practise pushing the ladder. At first it hardly moved, but she got better and stronger each time she tried.

They were ready. While he was out, they placed the ladder up to the attic entrance. Penny rehearsed what she would say out loud.

When he returned, she told him that she had been cleaning the attic and had found something truly disturbing – frightening and very scary.

She told him about the skeleton she had found. He laughed at her, saying it was probably a Halloween decoration, not real.

She begged him to take a look, as she was frightened. He said he would but not until he had eaten.

She tidied away the remains of their meal, and he said he was finally ready to see this "real" skeleton.

She was told to hold the bottom of the ladder and watched him slowly climb to the attic entrance.

Once he neared the top, Laura sprang into action and, straining hard, managed to push the ladder over.

He screamed as he fell and landed awkwardly. The ladder fell heavily on top of him. Thud!

Penny only just managed to step out of the way in time. She knelt beside him.

Watching her abusive husband take his last breath, she felt no guilt, shame or sadness.

She used his mobile to call an ambulance, making sure she sounded suitably distressed.

Laura watched from the attic. Ending the call, Penny looked up and smiled.

Penny told Laura she would immediately inform the authorities about her body.

She thanked Laura profusely for saving her sanity and her life.

Laura was only glad she was able to save Penny.

Especially as she had been unable to save herself.

The ambulance arrived. Then they alerted the police.

Dead End Tales

The police said accidents happen at home.
Her husband's body was quickly removed.
At last she was free.
Together they did it.
They had succeeded.
He was
dead.

Jane Pobgee

Jane Pobgee

Goodnight Eileen

Cathy Cade

"Why don't you sit down, Mum? I can do that."

The tea towel stilled in Eileen's hand. Crane-like, her gaunt neck lengthened, as if emerging from the customary dark silk scarf. She looked down her beak.

"I hope I can still manage a bit of drying up," she snapped.

Lara hadn't the temerity to contradict her mother. If she mentioned that swaying pause for breath, it would be dismissed as her imagination.

Her wet fingers tucked wayward hairs back in their clip. Upstairs, the children were quarrelling. Her husband appeared in the doorway, hair ruffled and glasses askew.

"Can I drop you home, Eileen, when I take the kids to Scouts?"

"Could you, Rob?" Lara replied before her mother had the chance. "That would be helpful."

A gust whipped hair into Lara's eyes. She shivered and refastened a shirt button that had pulled undone.

While Rob checked the children were strapped in, Eileen was exchanging pleasantries with neighbour Josie through the passenger window. The breeze caught Josie's curls when she stood back to wave the car off.

"Night Eileen."

Lara winced. Mum hated that. She thought their generation should address her as Mrs Harper.

The car turned the corner.

The sun came out again.

"She's a marvel, your mum," said Josie, "for her age. Is she still volunteering at the charity shop?"

"Two days a week," said Lara. "She can't just relax and let go," *of my life.*

"I see her here quite often."

She usually ignored Josie's prompts but today she needed an outlet.

"She's here most days when she's not at the shop. If she hasn't thought up a reason for me to collect her, she'll come on the bus. Rob says it would be easier if she lived with us." Even the thought of it exhausted her. "But she won't give up her bungalow."

Josie nodded. "Independent."

"Stubborn." She sighed. "Lately though, she seems... drained. She gets breathless though she won't admit it."

"Sounds like my dad; maybe her heart's playing her up."

"It wouldn't dare."

Eileen relaxed back on the sofa, clutching the remote control, although she hadn't yet turned on the television. It was so peaceful here, just drifting. She would get up and close the curtains in a minute.

Thoughts trickled.

She loved her grandchildren, but...

Lara and Peter had never been so loud, she was sure. There was no need for all that shouting and screeching.

Did one's tolerance of noise diminish with age?

She had less patience with everything these days: mugs that leaped out when she opened the cupboard, pens that slipped through her fingers, tiny impossible buttons, jars that wouldn't open... she supposed that was her hands, not the jars.

How could she keep control of her world when she couldn't control her own hands?

She had always been strong: in charge. Now nobody noticed her. Lara didn't listen and never consulted her these days.

She inspected the hand that held the remote control. Its nails were still strong and elegant although her shaky aim meant painting them took longer. Lumps on the knuckles were, apparently, arthritis, although they didn't hurt like her knee did. She moved her fingers and watched the tendons dance behind wormlike veins that bulged under withered skin.

She was drying up, like some shrivelled leaf, still recognisable but dehydrating. She imagined her desiccated husk lifted on a breeze, her home receding far below, and there was Lara's...

Drifting.

So peaceful.

The crematorium was full. Her brother's eulogy was moving, but Lara remained dry-eyed. Rob had told her she was too busy to grieve properly.

"You're not yourself, love. I'll take a couple of days off work to register the death and help with funeral arrangements."

She'd sent him in to work. She didn't want time to grieve.

Now, composed and indomitable, she received the condolences of people who'd known Eileen through her fundraising and charity work. She was glad they didn't all come back to the house. She'd only catered for family and friends.

Peter said, "It must have been a shock, finding Mum like that."

"Not at first. She looked as if she'd fallen asleep holding the TV remote."

It had felt like a cloud lifting. She pushed the thought aside. "Can I get you another cup of tea?"

Josie said, "You'll miss her. All those birthday cakes and halloween costumes, babysitting, helping out."

Organising, advising, disapproving. Taking over. "Yes. Mum's always been there."

And now she wasn't.

Peter's family were last to leave. She closed the front door and paused at the hall mirror to confirm that no hair had strayed from its appointed place.

"Mu-um, can we change out of these now?"

She adjusted the dark silk scarf at her throat. "Go on then. Make sure you hang them up."

"Yay!" The children pounded upstairs.

"Less noise, you two. There's no need…"

…to wake the dead. She'd stopped herself from completing the phrase.

Collecting a mug from the hall table, she surveyed the living room, where Rob was clearing plates and cups. In the kitchen, Josie had started on the washing up. Lara picked up a tea towel.

"You go put your feet up," said Josie. "We can do this."

The scarf's label poked at her skin; she stretched her neck to dislodge it.

"I'm fine," she snapped, hearing irritation in her voice but unable to control it. "I hope I can still manage a bit of drying up."

First published by Flash Fiction Magazine *at* *https://flashfictionmagazine.com/blog/2019/06/19/goodnight-eileen/*

Murder, She Said

Hilary Woodjetts

Now listen, children, carefully. Pay heed to my advice.
If you plan to do a murder, think it through. At least twice.
What's your motive? Is it jealousy, love, pride, or greed or lust.
Or p'raps doing it for someone else, if you really must!

Tools to use? There's poisons – multitudinous and various.
They can be instantaneous and make your victim nauseous
Before becoming fatal, giving ample time delay
For you to show a clean pair of heels as you get away.

What about a gun? Point blank, or sniper from afar?
The latter's a bit risky if your aim's not up to par.
The former choice is messy as blood spatters everywhere.
Burn your clothes, clean up the mess, and don't forget your hair.

Cleaning must be careful, meticulous, swift, yet patient.
Indoors pick up your casings, because of the striations.
(Each gun leaves a pattern, individual when it's fired.)
Leaving nothing for forensics, you'll only be admired.

What about an acid bath? Piranhas in a river?
Now that we have plastic baths, perhaps that's not a given.
Piranhas involve travel, but don't let that make you quiver.
Second honeymoon for us?' (Will fishes like his liver?)

Dead End Tales

You could use a knife – most kitchens have them handy in a block
To dispatch one or the other caught in unholy wedlock,
But I wouldn't recommend it; far too difficult to clean.
Besides which, you might spoil the set, and that's a bit too mean.

I am telling you this so that you don't make the same mistakes
I did back then. Back when your dad suggested we should take
That second honeymoon. I thought 'Not on your very life',
And picked one out so carefully – then stuck him with the knife!

And that is why, on Visitors Day, I give you this advice.
If you plan to do a murder, think it through… at least twice.

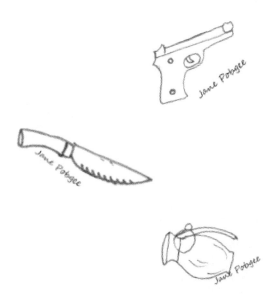

The Telescope Murder

Philip Cumberland

An excerpt from Philip's forthcoming sequel to Killing Time in Cambridge

Arnold's thought of having a quiet night in, watching the telly was rudely interrupted by the ringing of his phone.

He had decided to stay in his flat rather than at Sylvia's for the few nights he was on call this week. She said she would be calling in later. He fumbled for his phone and pressed the button to answer the call.

"Lane."

He listened to Sergeant "Fred" Flint for a few moments, then responded.

"Do we know the victim's name?"

Fred replied, "Doctor Adrian Bing, a cosmologist at Trinity."

"What was he doing at the Astronomical Association at this time of night? Don't say stargazing."

"Well, he was. It is a regular event for children every Wednesday evening during the winter until British

Summer Time starts. I have taken my nephew a couple of times."

"Okay, I will be at the station in a few minutes."

Arnold put on a hi-vis waistcoat, cycle helmet and trouser bands, then made his way down to the garage to retrieve his cycle. Soon he was locking it up to the cycle rack at Parkside. Fred met him as Arnold switched off the cycle lights, and they walked around together to collect the car. There, he removed his trouser bands and cycle helmet, throwing them on the car's back seat before climbing into the front passenger seat.

"Do we know what happened to him, Fred?"

"It seems he was strangled with the strap on his binoculars while he was answering a call of nature."

"Perhaps someone thought it was indecent exposure."

"No, it gets very dark just there in the field. When you move away from the screens, what lighting there is comes from red lights."

"So, is it a red-light district then?"

"No, they have to use red torches and lights so it doesn't mess up your night vision. They lock the main building up at eight o'clock, and when the big telescope isn't open, there are none of the usual offices available, so to speak."

The car pulled into the entrance, and a PC waved them along to the car park further down the road. Floodlighting was being set up as they walked towards three large screens, one lit by the image of a Windows screensaver. Two officers were taping off the area as they approached. Suddenly, a dazzling bright light lit the face of the late Dr Bing as a floodlight was switched on.

Arnold judged Bing to be in his late thirties, possibly early forties. Although it was probably a pointless exercise, they both pulled on plastic overshoes and gloves.

Jenny Read was standing by, waiting for the doctor crouching over the body to pronounce life extinct before she could start work. The young doctor got to his feet and declared Dr Bing to be dead. The pathologist arrived shortly afterwards and gave permission for the body to be removed.

Dr Bing's binoculars lay under him, the strap twisted tightly around his neck; at least, that's where Arnold assumed they were. He had thought they must be uncomfortable to lie on before remembering the man was dead.

"Can we turn him over, Jenny?" asked Arnold, as she seemed to have finished taking photographs of the body.

"Be my guest, but do it carefully."

It was when they were turning the body that they noticed the depression on the right side of the back of the head.

"I don't think he got that from the fall, Guv," said Fred.

"Nor do I. Do you want to get some pictures, Jenny?"

After Jenny Read had finished taking photographs, Arnold and Fred crouched down to have a closer look at the depression.

"That is a nasty bang. If that didn't kill him, I would think it knocked him out," said Arnold. "Have a look round Fred. See if you can find a weapon. Looking at the wound, it's probably a hammer."

While Fred was searching for the weapon, Arnold went through the late Doctor Bing's pockets. Although he found a mobile phone, a wallet containing cash, and a driving licence, there were no keys to either a car or house. Arnold picked up his phone and contacted the control room, telling them to find the victim's address and get a car there immediately. Also to find the details of any vehicle registered to the deceased.

He was conscious of Fred's torch beam searching the ground nearby. After a while the beam moved out of view.

It was a while before Fred got back to him, reporting that he hadn't found a hammer, but one of the people waiting to clear away the telescopes and equipment told him that one was being used earlier to knock in stakes for the rope cordoning off the equipment.

Most of the people at the event had left for home before the body was found. It was only after the clearing up was well under way that someone had spotted the body – a Mrs Geraldine Simpson. She was one of the organisers and a member of the society but not attached to the university. Arnold let Fred continue his search for the hammer and went to talk to her.

The lady, who Arnold guessed to be in her late forties or early fifties, was sitting in the entrance of an observatory. The area that housed the telescope was connected to the entrance hallway by a plain, windowless door. Logical, to keep the light out, thought Arnold for no particular reason. He glimpsed a wooden stairway through the door before turning his attention fully to Mrs Simpson.

"I am sure this has been a terrible shock for you, Mrs Simpson. Can you tell me what happened, how you discovered the body?"

"I was collecting up the cups and mugs. I make teas and coffees for the people putting on the show, so to speak. I couldn't see Adrian – he lodges with me. I give him a lift here. It's a bit dangerous for him to cycle in the dark. We live in town, Earl Street. I had just about finished collecting up the cups and was looking for Adrian. I was flashing my torch about near the screens. They were taking them down to put them away when I saw his body."

She started to shake with shock, recalling her experience, and sobbed.

"We didn't find any keys on his body, Mrs Simpson. Do you know if he had his keys with him?"

"Yes, he must have. He locked the house up."

Arnold excused himself. Promising to return, he phoned the station and asked someone to get around to Mrs Simpson's address sharpish and arrest anyone going into or coming out of the house. Arnold returned to Mrs Simpson, sitting down beside her, and resumed his interview.

"Is there anyone Dr Bing had fallen out with recently? Anyone you know of who wished him harm?"

She thought for a moment or two, then said, "No, not really. He was having a bit of a spat with a colleague at Kings, but nothing serious. You know what academics are like."

"What was the disagreement about, Mrs Simpson?"

"They are both, were both, working on using plants to generate electricity."

"I thought Doctor Bing was a cosmologist."

"He was, but he was doing a PhD in bio-electrical engineering. He was very clever."

"What on earth is that?"

"That's exactly what I said. My husband was a biochemist. He was a fellow at Kings. I lost the poor chap two years ago – hit-and-run along Newmarket Road. He had tried to explain it to me. Apparently, Adrian and Rory Jefferies were working on improving electricity production from plants."

"What?" exclaimed Arnold.

"My reaction too. It seems that some plants can produce electricity – not large amounts. The Dutch have been working on it. Adrian and Rory had found a way of significantly increasing the efficiency. They were about to publish and were squabbling over credit."

Arnold's phone rang; he excused himself to answer it.

"Lane."

He listened carefully to a police constable who had arrested a man leaving Bing's home carrying a laptop.

"Was the man Rory Jefferies?" He listened for the reply.

"Who was it then?"

The "who" was a local criminal working, it turned out later, for a major oil company. Rory Jefferies had also been attacked earlier that evening but, although badly injured, had managed to reach safety and was in hospital.

Following Footsteps

Jane Pobgee

It was dark, and she was tired as she stepped off the last bus at her stop. She almost missed her footing and would have fallen if not for a rough-looking man catching her arm. He stared at her but said nothing. She righted herself, thanked him and began walking home.

It started to rain. She wished she had stayed over at Katie's, but she had promised her mum that she would be back to look after the twins while Mum worked overtime on Saturday morning. She tried to help out whenever she could.

She crossed the main road and turned down the side street that led to her road.

As she turned the corner, she could hear tapping footsteps behind her. She slowed her steps to see if whoever was behind would pass; it could be just someone hurrying home. The footsteps slowed too. They were following her.

She sped up, not daring to look back. With her heart pounding, she heard the footsteps speed up too. Her breathing became more rapid, and her mind was in turmoil. What should she do? She imagined all sorts of things and none of them pleasant.

There were no lights in any of the houses she passed. She was too scared to stop and knock on a door in case no one answered, and the person following caught up with her.

She crossed over the road and, as she did so, tried to glance behind her to see who followed. She saw an empty street.

But they could be behind one of the trees that lined the street or someone's front hedge.

She stopped by the streetlight, and the footsteps stopped too.

She began walking again, a little faster this time. The footsteps kept up with hers.

She was terrified and began to cry, which made her even more breathless. Her throat felt as if it was closing up. She was nearly home; just one more corner to turn.

When she reached her own road, she thought she might make it home safely. The porch light came on as she approached her door.

It was then she noticed that one of the ankle straps on her gladiator sandals had broken. The footsteps she heard had been the brass trim banging on the pavement.

What an idiot she was, getting all worked up for nothing.

She let out a huge sigh of relief, just as a large hairy hand closed over her mouth and dragged her down the side alley between houses.

Highland Fling Brandon

Gwen Bunting

The light was fading early. It was only 2.30pm. Brandon would have to find cover soon.

He surveyed the surrounding hills, looking for any inlet in the hillside where he could spend the dark hours. He had been dropped by his Army unit in the Highland area of Morayshire, Scotland, on an officers' survival course.

He strode on towards a building in the distance. Through his binoculars, it appeared run-down and empty, with holes in the turfed roof, but it would be cover from the bitter January wind and shelter for the night.

He had limited provisions, so needed to use the skills acquired when he was a young boy in Ireland. In his kitbag was a dead rabbit he snared earlier that he would gut and roast when he was settled in the croft ahead. He increased his pace, anxious to see if the shelter was empty. He hoped to find a little wood inside the croft. Sometimes there might be a dead sheep inside.

Good! The croft was empty.

He switched on his forehead light as he entered, and something scurried away into the crevasses of the building. The roof was still intact in one corner. He slipped his kitbag from his back and pulled the ground sheet out, spreading it just long and wide enough for his body.

He looked around for the remains of a fireplace to use; his light skimmed the walls and settled on a hole in the wall. A fire had been lit at some point in the past, and a small stack of wood stood close by; that was a lucky find. Wonder who was here last? Perhaps skiers, or a shepherd out looking for lost sheep.

He rubbed the flint on the stone, and soon a spark lit the tinder, which he placed underneath the pile of dry heather. Soon the fire was ablaze, and Brandon added more wood, making a cooking rail for the rabbit he had just skinned and gutted to lie across the fire. He placed a sooty mug over the flames and poured water from his bottle to heat for a brew.

The wind was beginning to intensify, and smoke from the fire blew into Brandon's face. Coughing and spluttering, he leant back, overbalanced, and the mug of now scalding water spilled over his boot and leaked into the laces. Expletives flew from his mouth as he shook the wet boot. He began again, water in the mug…

In his billycan were wild garlic, mushrooms, herbs, and rice, which he proceeded to boil together. Fat dripped from the rabbit onto the flames, which crackled loudly. Brandon took the cooked meat from the skewer and dropped it into his billycan to eat. It reminded him of his days as a boy in Ireland.

As one of twelve children, there was never enough to eat, even when the old man was sober enough to go out poaching. Brandon learned many skills from his father and grandfather; they were never in favour of paying for anything that could be caught on someone else's land, whether legal or not. The only thing they could not get free was the booze, unless a still was going somewhere in the woods nearby.

The sweet tea tasted good. The honey helped, along with a chunk of dark chocolate he always carried to round off the meal. Unusually for a soldier, he did not smoke.

Before crawling into his sleeping bag, he left the croft to relieve himself. On the way back, he looked around for peat sods that would smoulder overnight while he slept. Back in the building, he added the peat to the now blazing fire; it quickly damped down. He did not wish to give his position away easily.

He slept soundly until suddenly, he awoke to shouts and sounds of people fighting! It took him seconds to come to his senses. Had the fungi he ate earlier made him hallucinate? It had knocked him out well and truly.

He sat up. Through gaps in the croft, he could see men dashing around. He heard guns blasting off and a language he vaguely understood. It was Gaelic.

The battle was in full force; men lay injured on the ground; women screamed for them to stop – clan fighting, it would seem. From his own knowledge of Irish Gaelic with its similar words, he deduced that a daughter of one clan wished to marry the son of a high-ranking member of an opposing clan.

Brandon stood up and went to the open doorway. No one noticed him; the battle continued. What should he do? He would only get killed if he tried to stop the massacre. Their dress was of Highland origin: the men in kilts with mantles hanging from their shoulders and swords flashing in the moonlight. It was like watching a film.

Brandon rubbed his eyes. No, there was no film crew around; just these men desperately trying to kill each other. He must be dreaming. Whatever was happening to him?

Suddenly a club thrown by one of the fighting men hit Brandon on his head, knocking him out.

He did not know how long he had been lying outside the croft. Standing over him a fellow soldier shone a light in his face.

"Who the f….. hell are you?" The light asked.

"Private Dungannon." Brandon scrambled to his feet, adding "sir" quickly.

"I am Sergeant Major Blanchard," he barked. "Stand to attention when addressing me, soldier."

Brandon came to attention and tried to explain.

"I bunked down here overnight and had a nightmare, I think. I saw these Highland men fighting, swords flashing in the moonlight, speaking what I can only say would be Gaelic."

"You were dreaming lad," the Sergeant Major barked back at Brandon. "We were camped ten miles away and heard nothing.

"Get your gear together, lad, and be on your way. We meet at Kilburn point at ten hundred hours. Look sharp, lad."

The Sergeant Major moved away to join the rest of the men, who stood laughing.

One of them mumbled, "Wouldn't mind a dram of what Brandon's been drinking. F****** cold out here."

Brandon quickly pulled his gear together and stuffed it into his kitbag, including a club-like piece of wood that lay just inside the door of the croft. He concealed it quickly before anyone might notice, it not being of Army issue. He would examine it more closely when he was alone. Checking his position with his compass, he started off in the direction of Kilburn while the rest of the group climbed aboard their transport.

Full daylight was still a few hours away. This part of the world did not see good light until 10am, and it was now only 6am. As soon as he was well out of sight of the Squaddies that found him, he would brew up. He had been lying outside for God only knows how long and was cold. He tramped a few miles and reached a crevice in the earth with a stream running nearby. After carefully looking around, he decided he would brew up here.

Pulling a few dry twigs from his pocket, he sparked his flint to ignite the tinder. At the nearby stream, he filled his water bottle from the foaming, fast running peaty water bound, he assumed, for a loch. While the fire heated his mug of fresh water, his thoughts returned to the dream, or nightmare, he experienced during the night.

Was it a dream? No, the wooden club piece he had picked up inside the croft bore blood stains matching the abrasion on his forehead. What could he deduce from what he saw and heard?

He arrived at his next check-in ahead of the Sergeant Major and his gang of onlookers. Kilburn was a small town with an Army Barracks. He reported to the Guard Room and was directed to the shower block and the hut he would sleep in that night.

The shower felt wonderful after being out in the field for three days and the bunk was reasonably comfortable.

He surveyed the room. It seemed he was only sharing with five other beds. His thoughts again began to relive the hoolie he had experienced a couple of nights back.

When off duty, he would have a look around Kilburn to look for information about the piece of wood that knocked him out.

Now his course had ended, and he awaited assessment results, Brandon had time off. Kilburn boasted a museum.

He entered it dressed in civilian clothing and looked around. A glass cabinet housed a few old kilts and brooches, but not much information about them.

He approached a man who looked like museum staff. Showing him the piece of wood, he asked if there was any chance of someone identifying the age of it, or what it may have been part of originally? He did not go into the story of how it came into his possession.

The man seemed interested. He offered the service of carbon dating the wood for a fee. Brandon decided to pay up and left an address to forward their findings after briefly explaining where he had found it, with a map reference.

He did not go into details of the "hoolie" he had witnessed.

The man gave a knowing smile and said they would be in touch.

A Ghost Story

Rita P Skeats

Someone knocks at your door. You open it to find your deceased grandfather who has come back from the dead to pay you a visit. What does he want?

Tom was jolted out of another bad dream, the spectre of his grandfather with sadness in his eyes, beckoning him to follow in his footsteps. He shuddered and put on the bedside lamp. He tried to read J R R Tolkien, but that conjured up nightmarish monsters. He must do something about the recurring dreams of his grandfather, Budhan. Tomorrow, he would speak to his younger sister, Mitra.

Mitra was more intuitive than Tom and dabbled in Tarot readings and other mystical practices. She did not have memories of her grandfather, for she had been a baby when he died. During one of her recent Tarot readings, the psychic told her that her grandfather wanted to communicate with her and described him as a well-dressed gentleman, wearing a Panama hat, smoking a Cuban cigar and singing Cuban songs, but she had turned down the request. She told Tom of her Tarot experience.

"That d-d-description fitted Grandfather," he stuttered nervously. "I will show you an old photograph of him."

He rummaged through an old chest of drawers and found a black-and-white photograph of their grandparents. How young they were, thought Mitra. Grandfather was dressed smartly and wearing a Panama hat. He seemed to stare out of the picture at them. It was eerie, and Tom quickly returned it to the drawer.

Tom was eight years old when Grandfather Budhan passed away suddenly. Tom was the favourite grandchild and had fond memories of his grandfather. Budhan taught him how to shoot with a bow and arrow and slingshots. He showered the boy with comic books and told him great stories of family history before and after his parents had emigrated from India. Tom had listened attentively and absorbed his grandfather's teachings. He had been inconsolable after the tragic and sudden death of the old man.

"Why am I having these recurring dreams of Grandfather bidding me to follow in his footsteps, Mitra," Tom bristled with nervous energy. "He passed away sixty years ago. It seems absurd that I keep having recurring dreams of him over the last two years."

"Yes, it seems to have started after our father passed away two years ago," agreed Mitra. "I think that there is a connection. You are the executor of Dad's estate, and we know that Grandfather Budhan's lands are held in a trust for his seven sons, including our dad. Now that Dad is no more, it is up to you to deal with the land issue."

Mitra's perception made sense to Tom.

Tom began the process of allocating his grandfather's estate as intended. He wondered why the land was held in a trust for over sixty years.

Tom did research into the land registration laws in Guyana and answered his question about the trust. If Budhan had not secured a trust, the Guyana government would have seized the land after he had died. He was indeed an astute businessman, thought Tom, and he felt a warm glow of Budhan's love wrapped around him. He was proud of his grandfather for protecting the family legacy.

He made several journeys from his home in New York to Guyana, his grandfather's home, putting into motion a number of projects that Budhan had discussed with him when he was a little boy. One of these was building a hotel on the family land by the sandy beach. That was also his father's dream, but it never materialised because of corrupt and undemocratic governments in Guyana during his father's lifetime. With Guyana going through a process of radical changes and the democratic government open to investments, Tom could now realise his grandfather's and father's dreams.

He would return and live in Guyana with most of the family. That's what Grandfather Budhan had wanted and, hence, the recurring dreams.

Tom can sleep in peace now. Occasional dreams of his grandfather are peaceful and happy, showing a smiling old man, Panama hat sat haughtily on his head, puffing away at a large cigar and waving to him as he disappears into the misty background.

Just a Terrible Accident

Jan Cunningham

I have always been a dreamer, right from childhood. And I could remember a lot of them. Once, I began writing them down in an exercise book. I've still got it somewhere.

But then I started to get recurring dreams, and I didn't like those. They were new to me, and I found them quite frightening. They always happened after I had become very angry with someone in real life.

Take the time when I was at senior school; I'd be about fifteen and dating the best-looking boy, Toby. We were the dream team. All the other girls were so jealous, saying nasty things behind my back. I didn't care. Then one Monday morning, a new girl joined our class. She had just moved into the area. I grant you she was stunning: long blond hair, ice-blue eyes and a curvy figure to die for. I hated her on sight. I'm not saying I'm not pretty, but we were complete opposites; I am slim, with long dark hair and chocolate brown eyes.

She stood in the doorway and surveyed the room, paying particular attention to the boys. She settled on my Toby, and I knew I'd have a fight on my hands. It took her a week of flirty glances in class, flicking her hair seductively whenever he came near and cutting me out in the café where a group of us went some evenings. She always managed to sit with him, pressing her thigh against his and looking adoringly into his eyes. When he dumped me for her, I was raging.

That's when the recurring dreams started. In it, she and I argued fiercely, with me shouting at her to leave Toby alone – he was my boyfriend – and she shouting that she always got what she wanted. Then I'd push her down a flight of stairs, and she was dead.

I'd wake up feeling awful. I'd have the same dream three nights running and then things went back to normal, and I could enjoy my dreams once more.

Several months later, we heard from the Headmistress that she had fallen down the stairs at home and broken her neck. The police could find no evidence of foul play, no signs of forced entry to the house, no other DNA than those of her family. They concluded that it was just a terrible accident. We were all stunned, but I didn't link it to my dream then. Why would I? It was ages ago and I'd forgotten all about it.

Years later it happened again at University. I was in my second year and had been seeing Max for at least six months. We were a couple in my eyes and my friends' until she came along. Felicia, 'call-me-Flicker', arrived on our campus part-way through the term. She transferred here because she and her parents had just returned from America, and the course she was studying was similar to one running at our University. She was tall, willowy, and very stylish. Her short, brown hair was expertly cut, her make-up was just enough, and her clothes were bang up to date with the latest fashion. Obviously, her parents were loaded, unlike most of the students who were strapped for cash and whose clothes mainly came from charity shops. It didn't take her long to decide Max was for her.

I tried. I made sure my long hair was always shining, I wore very little make-up and even splashed cash on a new outfit. All to no avail. She wheedled herself into our set, coming to the pub with us, always managing to sit next to Max, pressing her thigh against his… Swimming, she wore the tiniest bikini to show off her beautiful, tanned figure. She was an excellent swimmer. I hated her. In less than a fortnight, he was hers and who could blame him? Me! I was raging inside.

That's when the recurring dreams started again. This time Flicker and I were arguing over Max, naturally. Again, I wished her ill. I couldn't bear to see them together, holding hands as we used to, stopping to kiss every now and then. I became a virtual recluse, studying hard and taking myself off for long walks by the river or nearby woods. My heart was broken, and I was looking forward to the coming holidays so I wouldn't have to see them every day.

When we arrived the next term, we found out that Flicker would not be returning. We learned that she had drowned in the sea whilst holidaying with her parents. We found it hard to believe, as Flicker was a strong swimmer, but apparently one day she had swum out too far, got into difficulties, and the strong current carried her away. By the time anyone realised what had happened, the desperate measures taken to try to rescue her were too late. Her parents were inconsolable and couldn't wait to be allowed to bring her home for burial. Everyone, including the police, agreed it was a terrible accident.

We were informed of the arrangements for the funeral in case any of us would like to go and pay our respects. Max and some of the others went, but I couldn't face it. After my dreams of us fighting, I felt some sort of responsibility for her death.

Why? It was only a dream.

I made a pledge to myself that no matter what happened in my life, I would never allow myself to reach the pitch of the anger that caused the recurring dreams. I would master it somehow. And I did until...

The years passed, and I was happily married to Tom, a stockbroker. People said he was boring, but that's just how I wanted him. He was good-looking, reliable, steadfast and utterly in love with me. I had become quite a well-known writer and at times would have to go away for a few weeks on book-signing tours. The thought of Tom being unfaithful made me smile. Never in a million years; I trusted him implicitly. Why do you think I chose him?

We had a beautiful house in the country with acres of land. I love horses and riding, so we set up a small stable-yard and rented out the spare boxes.

My horse, Domino, was a handsome, coal black stallion who could be a handful at times, but mostly we got along fine. We employed a man from the village to come and work in the stables and look after the horses when we were away.

I made friends with several of the village ladies, especially those who enjoyed riding, and one or two would accompany me out on a ride sometimes. We all met occasionally for coffee or lunch where we held moaning or gossiping sessions, depending on our mood.

Dead End Tales

You will think me terribly naïve or just plain stupid not to notice what went on right under my nose, but I honestly didn't. I had such faith in Tom, it never crossed my mind. Anna, one of my horsey friends, began visiting her horse and our house more and more often. She seemed to be always around just as we were about to eat, and I felt I had to invite her to join us.

She was lovely, a do-anything-for-anybody kind of person. Her naturally curly, mousey brown hair suited her round face. She wasn't tall – rather dumpy in fact, but funny and good-natured. Not Tom's type at all.

When I next went on tour, I said to Anna, without thinking, "Keep an eye on Tom for me whilst I'm away. Make sure he doesn't get up to any mischief." I laughed, got in my car, and drove away.

On returning, as I was early, I decided to stop at the delicatessen near us and buy Tom a bottle of his favourite, expensive wine and a local blue cheese he was rather fond of. I envisaged his face lighting up as he saw me and when I showed him his gifts, he would smile and look knowingly at me. A meal with the wine and then to bed to catch up on the last week.

I left my car in the lane behind the house, to keep the element of surprise, and crept up the garden path to our kitchen door. When I looked in the window, I couldn't believe my eyes (I know you've all got there before me) but there were my husband and Anna, half undressed and in a passionate embrace. I was stunned. I crept back down the path and went and sat in my car.

What to do now? Well, she was not having him. He was mine. Then the rage began. I would fight for him.

I arrived back at the appointed time, giving nothing away. The evening progressed as usual, but the dreams began. I was arguing with Anna about Tom, wishing

62

her every evil I could think of. This time the dream didn't stop after three nights; it went on and on as my anger built to a crescendo.

One morning, I awoke early. As the dream faded, I decided to go for an early ride. I tacked Domino up and we trotted out of the stable yard onto the bridle path. My rage had reached fever pitch. I didn't know how to handle it, so I prayed that a hard gallop in fresh air would quell the flames and gave Domino his head. Suddenly Domino shied up on his hind legs, came down and began bucking. As I flew over his shoulder, the last thing I heard was Anna's voice.

"Two can play that game. Now he is mine forever."

When they found Domino quietly munching on the front lawn, a search party was arranged to search for Marcia. They found her eventually in a field near a hedge. She was dead. They surmised that Domino must have shied suddenly at something, catching Marcia unawares, and she had been thrown over his head and the hedge.

It was agreed that it was just a terrible accident.

Jane Pobgee

Reg

Philip Cumberland

Reg was lost; it wasn't an unfamiliar experience for him.

It seemed a strange town at first sight, but something about it was familiar. The light was fading, and the streetlights were coming on as the ones in the shops were being switched off.

The pub was well lit. Its light spilled out of the windows creating pools of light on the pavement below. He decided to give it a try. A girl – well, a young woman, probably in her early thirties – came out through the half-glass door and held it open for him. She was dark-skinned, her eyes a beautiful deep brown, but it was her hair that captivated him. It was jet black, just over shoulder-length, thick, and luxuriant.

He thought for a minute or two, pausing briefly just inside the door. As he got older, women became young women and young women, girls. Meanwhile, the man watching him shave in the mirror became daily older. This train of thought wasn't helping him.

He walked confidently up to the bar and ordered half a pint of draught cider. The barman was a man of medium height and build. He's got less hair than me, thought Reg. While paying for his drink, he asked the barman where he was.

"The Three Tuns, High Street, Huntingdon, sir."

It was like switching on a light. Reg suddenly knew where he was. He carried his glass to a table beside a window that looked out onto the road. The church was partly hidden by the building opposite, now offices. He cast his mind back to his childhood when the earlier building had been the gas showroom. Why had gas fridges fascinated him? He knew of them but hadn't seen them other than in the brochures. Or, if he had, he hadn't recognised them for what they were.

It was when he brushed hair back with his hand that he felt the egg-shaped lump on the back of his head and noticed it was painful. He hadn't been fully aware of the dull ache before; it was there, certainly, but it hadn't registered until he touched the lump.

Gradually his memory started to return. As it did so, the headache became more noticeable. It was refusing to be ignored now. He remembered driving to the town, parking up by the river in the long-stay car park. He had driven in through Hartford and remembered noting that the Sun pub was now closed and converted into a house. How long had he paid to park for?

He remembered entering his registration, putting money in the machine, collecting the change, displaying the ticket in the car on the dashboard, and then locking the car. How many hours had passed? Why was he here and how many hours' parking had he paid for?

The bump on his head troubled him, but he thought if he remembered why he was here, where he had been and who he had met, the cause of his sore head might become apparent.

Why he thought then of his mum he didn't know. Why her cooking, her weekly fruit cakes, roast dinners, and big fried breakfasts? Again, it had no logic. Reg began to feel hungry; perhaps it was the thought of his mum's cooking. He finished his cider and stepped outside the pub, where the smell of fish and chips intensified his hunger. He located the source of the smell, a chip shop near the pub, and within a few minutes was sitting on the low church wall opposite the chip shop eating his fish supper from the paper bag.

He remembered sitting on that very wall as a teenager waiting for the bus in the mornings to take him to work. There had been railings on top of the wall at one time; they had probably been cut off for wartime scrap. Their remains lay buried in the stonework.

Reg was enjoying his supper when a police car sped by, lighting the buildings they passed with flashes of blue light. Two more cars followed, both unmarked, then a white police van, and finally an ambulance. Reg turned to watch them turn off right and disappear out of sight. I wonder what all that was about, he thought?

He had noticed the blood on his left hand in the chip shop and surreptitiously grabbed a napkin from the counter to wipe the hand clean, putting the soiled napkin in his pocket. The chip shop owner, or at least the woman serving, hadn't commented on his head, so he assumed there was no blood. Just to be sure, he rubbed his hand over the bump and looked at it under the streetlight. It was clean, and his head hadn't felt sticky. It was really throbbing now. Still, he had paracetamol in the car and, he thought, a bottle of water.

Dead End Tales

He wiped his hands with another napkin, screwed up the chip papers, added the napkins and put them in a litter bin nearby. He set off along the road towards the car park, hoping that he hadn't overstayed.

It was as he was crossing the road that he saw the police in the car park, lit by the blue flashing light of the patrol car parked near the entrance. A white tent was being erected. The figures in white overalls didn't bode well either, he thought.

Reg crossed the road and walked into the car park.

A young, uniformed policewoman stopped him. "You can't come in, Sir."

"But I have come to collect my car."

She immediately became interested. "Which car is yours, Sir?"

"It's the red Fiesta near that tent."

"Would you wait here please, Sir?"

Reg started to feel uneasy as he watched the woman walk off in the direction of his car. She was back in a few minutes with an older man wearing a white plastic coverall, gloves, and shoe coverings.

"I'm Detective Inspector Cannon and you are. Sir?"

"Reg Oldfield."

"I understand you own the red Ford Fiesta over there, is that correct?"

"Yes, it's mine."

"Could you tell me about the body inside?"

"What body?"

Ghostwriter

Sandra Hughes

I could do with a ghostwriter writing for me,
But, unlike a Prince, I can't stump up the fee
For putting on paper the thoughts in my head
When my energy leaves me, and I'm stuck in bed.

Then I could get 'my truths' out there,
But lately I find I no longer care.
Let people believe whatever they like.
I'd rather my energy levels would spike.

There often are times when I haven't a clue
What to write on the themes that we're given. Do you?
My brain's empty of all except anecdotes
About pets with bad eating habits – or odd goats.

But I love the thought of collating my tales,
Leaving folk chuckling, hearing their wails
At times when life threw things at me,
But I could joke and make light, continue to be
Myself; while my stories are helping others:
Friends, sisters, fathers, mothers, and brothers.

Dead End Tales

Kind people have offered to help with this aim,
But I don't have the energy to fire my brain.
ME is the cause of confusion: brain fog.
And I've so many good tales about the dog!

You see, a ghostwriter would not write such twaddle,
But order my thoughts and make sense of the muddle,
My thoughts out of sequence and wrong memories
With incorrect dates or half-made-up stories.

Though I wouldn't use the same one as the Prince
As it seems he allowed things to go to print
Which, media-wise, really caused a kerfuffle.
And, in high places, stirred many a ruffle.
But I won't have a similar issue
As I don't frequent palaces. No one's left to sue.

But, again, like the Prince,
When my books are in print,
I will need to give them away,
(But not on planes, as on my bed I stay.)
Probably as presents for Christmas, birthday…
Well, any time really. Don't expect folks to pay.

Muse

Stephen Oliver

Well? Who is your Muse?

Ghostwriter

"Mr Richardson, what's your secret?"

The young reporter touched the button on the screen of his smartphone to start recording and laid it on the coffee table in front of him, next to the glass of excellent sherry.

His editor had sent him to interview Carl Richardson, the famous author. The man had a reputation for being able to write in the exact style and mode of any dead writer. People wondered how he did it. The cub reporter was supposed to find out.

"Please, call me Carl," his host replied. "What's your name?"

"My name? I'm Peter Charles." He smiled. "You might as well call me PC, like everybody else."

"Very well, PC." Richardson took a sip of sherry from his glass and settled back in the high-winged chair. "My secret's very simple. I steep myself in the writings of whichever author I decide to emulate next. I analyse their sentence structures, word choices, grammar styles, subjects, idiosyncrasies, etc. I set out to soak them up, to become them, in effect."

"That must take a lot of time and energy, Sir, … uh, Carl. Do you have any particular tools and tricks you use?"

Richardson smiled at him.

"I let my subconscious take care of all that, my boy." He took another sip of sherry. "All I need to do is spend several weeks reading and rereading everything I can get my hands on. Books, magazines, the author's notebooks, papers by university professors and students, whatever. It's all grist to my mill."

"Really?" Charles interjected.

"Of course." Richardson waved an arm around to indicate the bookcases lining every wall. "As you can see, I have a very extensive library. My first task is to accumulate everything I can find. First editions are excellent, of course, but if I can acquire the original manuscripts, so much the better. They're the real thoughts of the author, after all. Anything later has already been adulterated by the editors and others. I can't get a real feel for their way of seeing the world that way."

"Isn't that very expensive, Carl?"

He smiled again.

"Yes, it is. That's why I can only indulge myself this way since I've become famous."

"I see." Charles nodded in understanding. "People say that you've become much better in your later works. That would be the reason, I suppose. With all that information, you're that much closer to the authors and their minds, as it were."

"I absorb their spirits, so to speak." Richardson looked a little smug as he said this.

"Right." Charles nodded again. "How do you know when you're ready to start writing? Do you have a set time, or is there some other trick you have?"

Richardson looked thoughtful.

"I think it's when I feel as if I've become that person," he replied after a minute. "When I begin to think like they did, which will be very different from how I think normally, I know I'm ready. I sit down and start to write the stories I feel they wanted to tell before they died."

"Ah yes, about that," Charles said. "Why do you only write in the style of dead authors?"

Richardson looked a little self-conscious.

"I'm ensuring that there'll be no one to take me to court for plagiarism when I write something. Also, there's no chance they'll change their style, making it harder for me to emulate them. That would be very embarrassing. Their oeuvre has been fixed for all eternity."

Charles nodded again before changing the subject.

"One thing interests me personally, Carl," he began after a moment's hesitation. "Would it be possible to see your workroom? I've often wondered what it must look like."

Richardson looked blank for a moment as if unable to comprehend the question.

"Are you sure?" he asked, eventually. "I've always considered it an integral part of my method and, therefore, something to be kept private."

"All I want is just a peek. I promise I won't talk or write about it."

Richardson stood up.

"Very well," he said, "but I think you'll find that it changes your life more than you can imagine."

"I don't understand."

"If you follow me, all will become clear."

The two men walked down the corridor.

Richardson unlocked the door and opened it, ushering Charles in ahead of himself.

As his eyes adjusted to the room's dimness, Charles saw a desk to one side, equipped with a laptop, an old-fashioned typewriter, and what appeared to be a goose-quill pen and horn ink pot. Then he saw the vast circle that dominated the centre of the room, complete with lines and script in arcane languages he couldn't decipher.

He felt an unexpected prick in the side of his neck.

Although he didn't actually black out, he lost control of his limbs and senses for a while.

When he finally became fully aware again, he was still unable to move, but his senses cleared.

Richardson was in the process of tying his right arm to a post inside the circle.

"Ah, you're with us again," he remarked. "I didn't tell you the whole method, of course. That would be foolish because everyone could do the same, and I'd no longer be unique."

"What... What do you mean?"

"I imagine you took it as hyperbole when I said that I absorbed the spirits of the writers, but it's the literal truth. I've discovered a method to call up dead authors in such a way that I'm able to 'eat' their souls and take all their knowledge for myself."

Charles looked at him with a mixture of horror and amazement overlaid with confusion.

"I... I don't understand," he muttered.

"I don't suppose you do," Richardson replied. "I came across an old treatise which described the method I now employ. I no longer need to try to understand them by reading their works. All that guff I spouted before is totally irrelevant to me these days. Now, before I start writing, I call them into this circle." He gestured around them. "Once they've appeared, they're trapped, and I can absorb their essence. Then, I write."

Charles was unable to say a word. Instead, he began to struggle against the ropes binding his hands and feet.

"It's a most enjoyable occurrence," Richardson continued. "To have another man's life at one's fingertips, to be riffled through for its interesting little tidbits of experience, is a delight."

"You're nothing more than a vampire," Charles shouted, "living off the memories of the dead."

"I suppose I am. Not that that has anything to do with you."

"Then what's all this got to do with me?" Charles demanded.

Richardson smiled.

"For the best results, I need something to entice them here rather than forcing them to come. Eager ghosts are easier to eat and cause less indigestion." He paused a moment. "And the best thing of all is fresh blood and the departing life force of another human being."

He bent down and picked up a sharp dagger.

"Now then," he said as he lifted it high, "who shall I call up today?" He paused for a moment. "You know," he went on, "I've always wondered what really happened to Edwin Drood."

The dagger slashed down.

The Dreamer

Pearl Chester was fuming.

As the Chief Editor of the Chronicle, she could choose which reporter was sent on a particular assignment. This time, however, it had gone horribly wrong.

She'd always wanted to be a writer, not an editor, but had somehow never found the right words when she sat down with a pen and paper. Strangely, she could take anybody else's words and make them work. She just couldn't create anything herself.

For some years now, she'd suspected Carl Richardson was using supernatural, magical, or some other arcane means to enhance his abilities, but there had never been any proof. Even if there had been, discovering his methodology would have been next to impossible.

Then she met cub reporter Peter Charles when he started his first job with her newspaper.

Staff members made jokes about their having the same initials and asked if she'd ever had a love child. They even called him PC Junior. She'd stare at them as if questioning their sanity until they backed down.

No, it went deeper than that.

She quickly realised that they had precisely the same letters in their names. From her occult studies, she knew that this meant that there was a connection between them on a subtle level, according to the Law of Correspondences. From an esoteric point of view, they could be regarded as the same person.

She made use of this when she sent Charles to interview Richardson.

Before he left, she'd called him to her office, supposedly to brief him. The meeting had been utterly important. When she shook hands with him before he left, it allowed her to establish contact with him, transferring something of herself into him.

From then on, part of her had been riding behind his eyes, seeing and hearing everything he had but unable to influence him. She heard Richardson explain everything but discounted it. She knew that there had to be more.

She was delighted when Charles asked to see Richardson's workroom of his own accord. Now, she'd learn his secret.

Then it all went wrong when Richardson drugged Charles. Being in connection with him, the drug affected her too, narcotising her body, slumping over the desk in her office.

Only when he could struggle against his bonds could she wrench herself free of him mere seconds before he perished.

She sweated as she realised the danger she'd been in.

If Charles had died with her still inside him, she might have died too, as a worst-case scenario. The best case would have meant that she lost part of her mind and soul, rendering her incapable of functioning properly.

She knew now that Richardson was a necromancer who also practiced human sacrifice, a potent and evil combination.

And she still had no idea how he was calling those dead authors up.

She straightened herself up and walked to the curtained-off area at the back of the office. This was officially a sleeping space for her if she worked late, but she'd refashioned part of it into a sorcerer's workroom.

She sat down at her work table and took the necklace off her neck. When she slotted the jewel hanging from it into the space under her crystal ball, the ball clouded and began to emit light.

She directed it to show her the memories of the past hour, from when Charles arrived at Richardson's house. Step by step, she followed him once again until he walked into the room with the magic circle. She stopped the replay at that point and focused her attention on the circle itself. Inspecting every line and glyph took quite a while because she memorised everything.

There was something familiar about the configuration, but she couldn't quite put her finger on it.

She watched the memory strand almost to the end before stopping it again to examine the dagger.

No, it looked normal enough — just another ritual dagger, such as she owned by the dozen.

Blanking the crystal and removing the necklace took but a moment. She sat back and thought.

What is it about that circle that's so familiar? she mused. *Where have I seen it before?*

In an attempt to remember, she let her eyes wander over the bookshelf with all the grimoires she'd collected over the years. Some she'd bought at hideous expense; others were faithfully reproduced from yet older copies; yet more she stole, often at the cost of the previous owner's life. She'd never scrupled at anything that allowed her to increase her knowledge of the occult.

Her eyes were drawn to one small folio on the bottom shelf. It was something from her earliest days when she'd been a mere acolyte of the great Artus Pendragon. That was before she escaped becoming yet another sacrificial victim in his centuries-long search for the *Liber Noctis*.

She drew it out and carefully turned the pages, scanning each one with care.

I was right! she thought. *I knew I'd seen something like it before.*

She carefully read her longhand notes, marvelling at how little her handwriting had changed over the decades.

How to raise ye Spirits and become One with ye Dead and call Others Who have never yet died.

That was what she'd remembered.

As always, she read through the instructions three times with care. They were simple enough, although a note at the end contained a warning: *Decide with Care whom ye call. An exact Definition is vital.*

She was already sure who she wanted to call up, so that wouldn't be a problem.

The magic circle would have to be in the centre of her office; no other place would do because it was the only area large enough. Fortunately, she'd always favoured parquet floors, so there was no need to move any carpets — just a couple of chairs and a rug.

The circle took only a few minutes to draw, but the lines and glyphs cost her nearly half an hour because she needed to be exact in their placement and writing. A mistake could have ghastly consequences.

Once everything was prepared, she donned her mage's robes and stood just to the side of the central circle, trembling with excitement.

Holding her notes in her right hand, as the ritual demanded, and her best ceremonial dagger in her left, she began to chant the arcane words. She was very careful to pronounce them accurately because a slip of the tongue might cause the spell to fail. A bigger mistake could cause such a backlash that her very life and soul would be in danger. So, she was very conscientious indeed.

As the rite progressed to its climax, she came to the point where she had to name the spirit she was summoning. She wanted to speak with, in her mind, the greatest horror writer in the world.

"I call upon the Shade of Howard Philips Lovecraft, sometimes called the 'Dreamer of Providence.' I would fain speak with thee and thy Muse. I seek to commune with the greatest Dreamer who has ever been. Come to me. I call you with the baleful Names of Abaddon and Ahriman and Put Satanachia. I call you with the sublime Names of Elohim and Ahura Mazda and Gabriel. You will come to my Command. Come!"

The last word was screamed as she gashed her forearm with the knife, allowing a few drops of blood to fall into the circle before her.

As they landed on the floor, a faint smoke-like mist rose into the air, swaying like a cobra before it struck.

Slowly, the face part rearranged itself into the lantern-jawed image she'd seen so often on the fly covers of his books in her extensive collection.

A whispering voice spoke from the mist.

"Who calls me? Who disturbs the peace of the dead?"

"I do," she replied. "I am a magister and a Power in the world of the arcane. You will obey me in every possible way."

"*I can do no other*," the figure said. "*But beware. You know not what you ask of me.*"

"I know what I want. I want to discover how you wrote such compelling stories. I wish to find your muse."

"*You don't comprehend the danger of what you wish. Turn back now, before you suffer a like fate to mine.*"

"There's no turning back." She raised her dagger, which now glowed with eldritch energies, and pointed it at him. "You'll tell me right now, or I'll blast you and destroy you utterly!" she screamed.

"*I've but one thing to say.*" Lovecraft's ghost drew itself upright. " '*Ph'nglui mglw'nafh Cthulhu R'lyeh wgah'nagl fhtagn.*' "

"What did you say?" Pearl knew what it meant but couldn't believe he'd said it.

" '*In his house at R'lyeh, dead Cthulhu waits dreaming*'," the spirit repeated in English.

Even as he spoke, she could feel a more powerful Presence approaching. One neither benign nor baleful, but instead supremely indifferent to the concepts of right and wrong, as conceived of by mere human beings.

"**Who calls to Cthulhu and seeks to awaken Me?**"

Those weren't the precise words spoken, nor were they spoken by any human throat.

To her horror, Pearl understood them perfectly.

The language was R'lyehan, a tongue that had been dead millions of years before dinosaurs had graced the Earth.

She fell to her knees in terror.

The thoughts of the Presence were now in the room, unseen and unheard, yet their force and power made her head swim.

Lovecraft appeared to be bowing to it before turning back to the now gibbering woman.

"Did you not realise that I was but a mortal dreaming the dreams of He who, even now, lies dead and dreaming in His home under the sea? He is the greatest Dreamer of all. I made my bargain with Him to become a writer, and now He seeks a new vessel to pour full of His visions and reveries. You will be His new prophet. Remember: 'That is not dead which can eternal lie, And with strange aeons, even death may die.'"

The shade bowed again to the godling Pearl had summoned before beginning to fade.

"I go now and merge with the nothingness that is the true heart of reality. Farewell, although I doubt that you will enjoy the experience. No more than did I."

With a last wave of a misty hand, Lovecraft was gone.

Pearl was left alone with Cthulhu.

Soon, she'd be ready to write whatever He wanted her to.

She'd become a great author, as had always been her heartfelt wish.

Even now, she could feel the madness of His thoughts growing inside her.

The Paperhanger's Tale

Gwen Bunting

They left the crematorium and walked around the building to view the flowers for the late Jeff Shardlow who came to an abrupt end at the age of forty-nine.

Myra his wife, looked drawn and haggard after the coroner's inquest into Jeff's death. It had taken several weeks before they finally released the body for the interment. His cause of death was complicated.

Jeff posted advertising literature on enormous billboards around the city. He originally trained as a house decorator in his youth but, sadly, a change of fashion for home decorating led to less wallpaper and more painting over existing anaglyptic wall covering.

He enjoyed the freedom of the road. The firm provided him with transport, which he also used in his own time, adding more fuel. He often picked up private jobs from lonely, widowed ladies who needed a change of scenery in their homes. Sometimes it led to more than hanging wallpaper.

His own marriage was not as exciting as he would have liked, so the odd lonely lady brought more than just extra cash to his bank balance.

"Come on, Mum. Let's get into the car," Anna called, trying to steer her mother away from the flowers.

"Will be with you in a moment," Myra replied. "Just want to speak to Denise."

Myra shared a car with her daughter, Anna, and son-in-law, Marc, to drive to the house Myra and Jeff bought so many years ago. Anna had left the family home as soon as she was eighteen. Her father being so possessive and controlling, meant that Anna found work outside the area and lived alone until she met Marc.

Myra had employed a caterer to supply refreshments for any mourners who came back. She felt sure her in-laws would be first at the door.

The caterer opened the door on their arrival, quickly followed by Jeff's parents.

Myra settled into her favourite armchair, feeling glad it was all over, bar the Will reading, etc. That would be a surprise to all who were not invited to listen to the solicitor.

As she sipped a hot, sweet cup of tea and nibbled on a dainty sandwich, the in-laws crowded around her.

"Err, what time is Mr. Charlton coming to read the Will?" was her mother-in-law's first question.

"That will be in private, tomorrow, when just Anna and I are present," was Myra's quick response.

"Oh, I thought you would want us there. Jeff always kept us in touch with what he did regarding his life," said the senior Mrs Shardlow.

"Well, this time he did not, and it only concerns Anna and myself." Myra responded rather curtly.

"Oh, I understand dear. Father and I only want to help and advise you," her mother-in-law responded, clearly hurt at having her nose put out.

The wake continued, with everyone speaking highly of Jeff, without knowing him at all. Jeff would have been most upset at having all these people in his home; he only ever wanted his close family to visit. Half these people from his past, Jeff would have ignored.

The guests started to leave. Anna and Marc began helping to clear up, but the caterer had it all in hand.

"We will be going then, Mum," said Anna, approaching Myra. "Will you be alright?"

"Of course, I will. Been on my own before love." Jeff was often away on business, as he called it, but Myra knew differently. Perfume lingers on men.

"Go home and see to my grandson. He will have missed you."

Myra poured herself a gin and tonic and settled once again into her favourite armchair.

This was the beginning of her new life. How she was looking forward to being alone and going where she wanted whenever she wanted. Suddenly, the doorbell rang, startling Myra. Who could it be?

Peeping through the spyhole, she saw her dearest friend, Denise. She flung open the door and embraced her, dragging her inside the house. How pleased she was to see her.

Denise had been present at the service, but only for Myra's sake. She would not come back to the wake but preferred to wait till all had gone. Denise never came to the house while Jeff was alive. He had made it clear she was not welcome at his home. Should she wish to see Myra, then meet her up town, not here! And that was how their friendship continued over the years.

Myra was delighted to welcome Denise into the house and quickly put a G&T in her hand. They raised their glasses to celebrate the death of Jeff. Their plans to help him slip off the ladder seemed to have worked, although it was worrying when the coroner took so long to release the body for cremation.

The fish glue Myra put on his shoes to ease the hard leather outer shoe slowly dripped into the sole until it gradually became more flexible. Jeff noticed only that his shoes were more comfortable than they had ever been. Until he climbed his ladder.

Jeff had brittle bones, and the fall broke his neck.

It helped that, on cold days he would have a quick nip of whiskey before ascending his ladder to paste up a SpecSavers advert or whatever he had been given to cover the boards. Later, when he had pasted his quota for the day, he would slip off to Mollie's for a cuppa and anything else she had on offer. This time, she had been left standing.

Jane Pobgee

The two stories that follow

(The Day the Laughter Died and *Lakeside Reflections)*
were written to a spooky photo prompt.
Here we have substituted a drawing,
to avoid copyright violation.

Jane Pobgee

The Day the Laughter Died

Wendy Fletcher

Sophie stared into the still water of the pool.

Diverted from the river at the edge of her grandparents' estate, the pool had many tales to tell.

Old photographs show pool parties at the end of the last century, when the ladies carried parasols and were accompanied by men in striped blazers. These photographs were rarely brought out now and Sophie's memories were blurred.

She was four when she last visited the pool, the day the laughter died.

What had she seen?

What had she heard?

What did she remember?

The grownups rushing down the sloping lawn to the water's edge. Her mother screaming. Then the hushed voices as she was ushered back to the house and handed over to Nanny Polly.

Where was Clara?

Why wasn't she brought back to the nursery?

Then came the realisation that photos of Clara got older. No new ones took their place on the side table in the drawing room.

Only now, as a grown-up eight-year-old, did she decide to make her way back to the pool.

Unobserved from the house, she skirted the ornamental gardens and pushed through the growth over the path to stand again on the edge of the pool.

In the silent water she saw the reflection of Clara and herself.

Now she understood. This privilege of watching her sister grow up was hers alone.

Only she could look into the still water, or a mirror, and see both of them as they developed and aged together.

For her parents and the rest of the family, Clara would always be the four-year-old whose life had ended the day she drowned in the pool and the laughter died.

Lakeside Reflections

Jane P and Cathy C

Angela looked at the gravestone her parents had placed on Annette's grave. It was a plain cross on top of a fairly plain stone with Annette's name, date of birth and date of death. It simply said, "Sleeping with the angels."

Angela knew this wasn't true. She was sleeping with the fishes. Annette had drowned in the Manor House fishpond. Although it was more like a lake than a pond.

Today she turned away from the gravestone and faced the small lake nearby. She walked to the edge and stared at her reflection, waiting for her sister to appear. She always did. Standing next to her reflection was Annette.

Angela spoke to her, telling her what she had been doing during the past week at school and how her parents were keeping. The rows and blaming each other were beginning to lessen, but they were still over-protective of Angela, hardly letting her out of their sight. Even now they were sitting on a bench not far away, watching her like hawks.

Annette sympathised with Angela and soon they were chattering away just like they used to. Eventually Annette asked Angela if she would do something for her, something that could be dangerous but would help her parents. Of course, Angela said yes, as she would do anything for her twin sister. They arranged to meet that very night at midnight by the Manor House fishpond…

The grandfather clock back in the hall began to strike midnight.

Angela squeezed through the gap in the fence behind their shed, and the tolling receded as she ran across the Manor House lawn and past the memorial to reach the edge of the fishpond.

Annette was there, waiting for her, as always. Her hand reached out of the water, inviting, and Angela took it, trusting. Of the two, Annette had been the leader, initiating their adventures and protecting her little sister, who was younger by almost two hours.

Now she drew the trusting Angela down into the water. In a very short while, Angela found she could not hold her breath any longer, and tentatively inhaled. To her surprise, her lungs accepted the water as if it were air, and she found she could breathe as easily as the large carp that swam around them. Annette swam easily, although she never learned in life, while towing her sister with one hand to the far end of the small lake. Here reeds lined the banks, and a willow tree overhung the surface. Here among the reeds, tiny people with arms and legs, like humans, but scales and gills, like fish, waited to receive them in the watery light of the full moon shining through the ripples.

"Welcome, Angela, sister of Annette."

The voice was in her head. She opened her mouth to reply, but only bubbles emerged. The tiny people laughed, producing bubbles in their turn.

Annette's eyes smiled at her. "Just aim your thoughts toward us, Angela, and we will receive them."

So Angela did. "Thank you for your welcome, but who are you?"

"We are mirlings. We live in this pond and want to thank you for allowing your sister to join us."

"Me? I had no wish for Annette to drown."

"She fell while trying to retrieve the doll you dropped. Had you not cried so at the loss of your doll, she wouldn't have reached so far and overbalanced."

This was not what Angela wanted to hear. She had banished the guilt that arose whenever she recalled that afternoon and had almost managed to convince herself that she hadn't driven her twin to such an extreme. Tears that had fallen so freely for the loss of her doll had since deserted her, as if some barrier held them back from releasing again.

One of the mirlings reached out her hand.

"Please don't be sad. Annette has come to teach us about humans so that we can better avoid their notice and live safely here in the pond, tending our fish. We value and honour your sister."

"They are very kind to me," Annette confirmed, "and I have become fond of the fish that share our pond."

When Angela heard her sister calling it "our pond", she knew Annette was happy here, away from the embroidery lessons she hated, and their father's rules that she didn't so much disobey as forget.

"But why have we never seen mirlings in the pond?"

Annette replied. "We stay out of sight when people are near, afraid of being caught in a net by curious humans. Like the fish, mirlings will die out of water, but it would be even worse to be kept in a fish tank and displayed like freaks in a fairground exhibit."

Angela nodded her understanding. She looked around at the mirlings, who seemed nearer her own size than when she first arrived. She realised that the fish seemed bigger too – or were she and Annette shrinking to mirling-size?

"Will I ever go home again? Or must I stay here with you?"

She had never been as adventurous as her twin. Angela was perfectly happy learning the things that bored Annette, like embroidery and piano playing.

"That is up to you, Angela. If you wish, you can stay here with me and the mirlings and swim free with the fish. Or you could go back to your life above with its petticoats and lace and the prospect of husband and children and housekeeping and Sunday services and afternoon teas."

It was clear from Annette's tone what she thought of those… but her eyes were sad, because she knew her sister well. To Angela, all the things Annette hated didn't seem boring, but familiar and cosy and safe. Unlike her twin, Angela looked forward to growing up and being like their mother.

So the sisters returned to the far side of the pond, where the moon hung over the memorial, and by the time they reached the other side, their heads almost reached the water's surface. Annette retrieved Angela's doll from under a waterlily and handed it to her in parting.

And Angela found she could cry after all. Great heaving sobs rose from her chest, choking her in a way that the pond water had not, until she found herself drowning in her own tears. The watery moon above them disappeared and her world turned black. Eyes screwed shut in her efforts to breathe, she felt Annette shaking her shoulder, and heard her calling her name.

"Angela, Angela… wake up, dear!" It was her mother's voice, after all.

Father's sounded brisker. "Come on, Angela. It's only a dream. Stop crying now."

"No, George. Let her cry." Mother sounded almost relieved. "She needs to cry."

And Angela couldn't stop crying until Father had gone back to bed and Mother had sung her a lullaby from when they were small, remaining at her bedside until Angela fell into exhausted sleep.

Only then did their mother rejoin her sleeping husband, leaving the lamp burning low. So intent had she been on comforting Angela, she still hadn't noticed the soggy doll propped against the bed's footboard, its eyes peeping out above the rumpled coverlet.

Read more about the mirlings in Pond People, *available from Amazon, Smashwords and other outlets found at* https://books2read.com/pond-people

How Many?

Val Chapman

"I'm sorry mum, I didn't mean to do it this time. It was an accident, honestly. I didn't mean to kill her."

Alice held her daughter tight and stroked her hair.

"It's ok, it's ok, we'll get it sorted."

Suddenly she stopped, put her hand on the girl's shoulders and looked down at her beautiful, tear-stained face.

"Wait... what... *This time*? What do you mean *this time*? You didn't have anything to do with the death of Father Paul, did you?"

Megan said nothing and simply looked at the floor.

"No. I don't believe that. Tell me you didn't." Alice was shocked. She had always wondered about the sometimes violent outbursts of her daughter's moods. She was a "complicated" child, after all, but surely it could never have gone this far?

"OK, right, let's sit down. I'll call Dad and we can talk it all through and decide what to do."

A short while later, the three of them were in the kitchen. Megan and her mother sat opposite one another, arms stretched across the old oak table, gripping each other's hands, while Dan, Megan's father, paced the floor.

He took a deep breath and sat in his usual seat at the head of the table.

"Right, let's go through this from the beginning."

Megan looked at him. "Do you mean Miss Williams or Father Paul, or..?" her voice trailed off.

Alice and Daniel looked at each other and back at Megan.

"What do you mean, *or*? Who else is there?"

"Well, Ryan kept on goading me, pretending he knew about Father Paul, and I'd just had enough."

"Ryan? Ryan? He isn't even missing, let alone dead. How can you mean, Ryan? He is away camping in the woods. Isn't he?"

"Well, he's in the woods, but he isn't camping."

This was escalating quickly. The two parents listened to their daughter calmly confessing to the murder of three locals, including her teacher and the local vicar, although Megan still maintained that the death of teacher Daphne Williams was a freak accident.

Her reasons were incomprehensible to Alice and Daniel, her methods both diverse and unbelievable.

They had been talking for a while. The summer sun had faded and cast long shadows through the house. Daniel looked up from where he had been sitting with his head in his hands and noticed that the hallway was illuminated by blue flashing lights and car headlamps.

He stood quickly. His daughter flung herself at him.

"Daddy, Daddy, tell them it wasn't me. Help me Daddy, please."

There was a slight pause. A voice called out and a round of applause burst through the silence.

The director walked over to the kitchen table and addressed the three people standing before him.

"Well done, everyone. Get yourselves home for the night and hopefully we can wrap up this episode of Midsomer Murders tomorrow. Good work, guys, and thank you."

Jane Podgee

Safe

Jane Pobgee

As the door slammed behind her, she leaned her back against it and took a few deep, calming breaths. When she felt able, she moved deeper into the small room. She felt safe when the door was locked.

She had almost been caught this time and got away by the skin of her teeth. She could still feel her heart thumping erratically. She sat on the bed in the corner and slowly went over everything in her mind, looking for where she may have made mistakes, left evidence. She knew this time there would definitely be some.

She regularly watched police shows on crime and forensic evidence and taught herself a lot about how to avoid leaving DNA in hair or skin cells. She took precautions before she left her bedsit. She made sure she exfoliated, showered, and dressed in nondescript dull clothes that she bought from charity shops. That way, when she returned she could burn them if necessary. Nothing at home could connect her in any way to the murders.

It had all started with an accident. She hadn't meant to kill him, but when she was pushing him off her, he fell

97

and hit his head on an iron fender. She actually saw the light go out in his eyes.

Realising he was dead, she tried to think carefully and calmly about what to do next. In his kitchen, she found bleach and added it to a bowl of hot water to wash any trace of her off him. She then proceeded to go over everything she had touched, washing off fingerprints or any DNA she may have left. She even vacuumed the rooms she had been in and emptied the contents of the vacuum into a carrier bag she found to take away with her. Once she was satisfied that no trace of her remained, she carefully took her leave. No one had seen her enter, and no one saw her leave.

Over the next weeks and months, she scoured newspapers and watched the news religiously, but apart from the report of his death, there was nothing. In time, she stopped worrying about it, stopped scouring the newspapers and watching every news bulletin. She had nothing to worry about.

She felt good – almost happy. In her mind she had decided he deserved it. After all, if he hadn't pounced on her, she wouldn't have needed to shove him off and he wouldn't have fallen and hit his head.

Life got back to its usual rhythm. She chatted with friends on WhatsApp and Facebook, signed on the dole each week, and went out occasionally for a drink. If she was honest, she was bored.

On the way home one night, after having a drink at the pub on the high street, a car pulled up as she waited at the bus stop, and a man she didn't know offered her a lift. She knew the risks of being picked up by a stranger, but at least it was a little excitement. She accepted with alacrity; it was a cold night, and the car looked warm. They chatted a bit, and he suggested she might like to go back to his for more drinks and to 'get to know one another'.

She knew exactly what he meant. She also noticed the light imprint of a ring on his finger, which had obviously been removed recently. So, she played along as if it was the best offer she'd had in ages. He became a little touchy-feely as he drove to his place; she didn't try to stop him. She could see he thought he was on to a sure thing.

His house stood on its own at the end of town. He pulled straight into the garage, and they entered through a door in the garage that led into the kitchen. He poured very large drinks for them both, and they moved into the living room.

She saw a photo on the sideboard, of a woman and two young children; she couldn't resist asking who they were. He told her it was his sister and her kids. She didn't believe him, but played along as if she did. He put on some romantic music and patted the seat beside him for her to snuggle up.

After some kissing and petting, which she quite enjoyed, he suggested they go upstairs. She said she wanted to stay downstairs as she liked having sex in unusual places, not boring old bedrooms. His eyes lit up, and she knew he was getting excited.

She asked if he had a downstairs loo as she needed to go. He pointed in the direction of the kitchen and said the cloakroom was just through there. She promised him she would not be long and went into the kitchen.

There she chose a knife from the knife block. Hiding it behind her, she returned to find him stretched out on the settee, naked as a jaybird. She laughed and said she saw he was pleased to see her.

She leant over him to kiss him. As he closed his eyes, she struck, just once, straight through the heart. He looked shocked, took a breath and died almost instantly. Ha, she thought. That will teach you to play away.

Once again, she sought out the bleach and cleaned him off, not just externally, but in his mouth as well. She wanted to make sure no bodily fluid had been exchanged. She went through the same process as before, and when she was certain she had cleared every trace, she left the house – not through the garage this time, but through the back door and across the field at the back. It took a while to get home, but she didn't mind as she knew she could sleep in tomorrow morning.

For the next few days, she once again read all the newspapers and watched the news. This time the death was reported as a murder. The police requested information and witnesses to come forward. She still felt pretty safe. The only person to have seen her was dead, and dead men tell no tales.

As the months passed, the police were no further forward and life became boring again. She decided she needed a night out. She chose a different pub this time. After a couple of drinks, she left to wait at the nearest bus stop.

This time she came equipped. She didn't know where she might end up, and she wanted to be sure she had a strong, slim blade with her. She let one bus go by and decided that if nothing happened by the time the next one came, she would go home.

Almost at once, a car stopped. The guy wound down his window and offered her a lift. She looked him up and down, decided she could risk it, and got in the car.

She'd pretended to be a little drunk and told him she had been celebrating getting a new job. He was full of all the chat and slid his arm around her as he drove.

She asked him where he lived. He told her not far, and within a few minutes was turning down a small side street of terraced houses. He stopped outside one, helped her out of the car and supported her into the house. Settling her on the settee, he told her he would get them drinks.

She heard him in the next room, talking on his mobile. He was talking about her, saying she was pretty drunk, and his mate should join them, as she was in no state to say no to anything. If someone else turned up, she would be in danger.

She immediately ran into the kitchen and stabbed him. Unfortunately, he was in the process of turning, so she didn't strike him exactly through the heart, and he tried to fight her off.

She knew she must go; his mate might not be far away. There was no time to do anything now but run – straight out of the house and as fast as she could.

Someone shouted after her and began to chase her. Fear lent her wings. She flew down the road and put a great distance between her and her chaser, finally making it home.

Safe.

Or so she hoped.

The news was full of the attack. This time, they had a description of a person of interest.

It was a pretty good description too.

In no time, she was arrested and came to trial.

It did not go well for her. Found guilty, she was sentenced to life, locked safely away in prison.

Jane Pobgee

Running Tide

Henry Curry

I've not walked here before. There's a sharp bite to the wind. I'm not sure I've ever had a "whetted knife"; all I know is that I'm glad I put a waterproof jacket on over my fleece. I have warm gloves on and a ridiculous woolly hat, but I still feel the cold, a lot more than in my younger days.

The salty spray whips up from the small wave crests, foaming the top of the creamy-white breakers. I feel a different sort of chill: the old melancholy of lonely strand lines and miles of empty beach. Not sad though, just reflective. Introspective.

Grand steam leviathans are casting their dark shadows across a deep blue sea, and I feel the fiery sunshine warming the land. Uplifting – yes, definitely uplifting. A black-headed gull expertly wheels across my view, screams, draws closer and then lands near me. I can't help but stop and marvel at its grace and then smile at the comical little red feet as it puddles in the sand. We observe one another for a little while. I'm convinced he is friendly – on some level we're communicating. Something spooks him, so he effortlessly lifts into the air and simultaneously defecates, narrowly missing me.

There's a change; only a few blue scars on the face of the sky now, and shafts of sunlight blaze like searchlights, creating a magnificent seascape. As usual, I can hear music playing in my head. Something in the rhythm of the waves has triggered a tune. Damn, I'll be whistling that for the rest of the day.

I look down as I walk along and play the game where I try and guess whether the tide is coming in or going out. Yes, the water came in a little further; there's the characteristic line. Tide's certainly on the way in. Or on the turn? But the next wave trickles in and stops a little farther back. I never do well at this game, but it passes the time.

It's then that I notice the small, light footprint in the wet sand just ahead of me. I am intrigued, since I haven't seen another soul on the beach. And, by rights... well, shouldn't the waves have washed this away?

Okay, that's interesting, there's another. I stop whistling and walk quickly forward, looking for more. Something makes me pause and look up, scanning all around, but there's no-one, not a living thing in sight, not even my friendly gull.

The sky is turning a heavy grey and is featureless now. I walk on again, studying the sand minutely, but there are no more footprints. I stop again, straining to listen. Somewhere on the wind there's a sad, sighing noise. I'm reminded of the old tales of sirens calling to sailors, wrecking ships with their alluring, haunting cries.

Now there's an odd aroma mixed in with the saline tang of the sea air. It's not altogether unpleasant, just out of place – odd. I'm trying to work out what it is when my attention is taken by a boat on the horizon, quickly getting closer. Where did that come from?

I can make out more features now. It appears to be an old cutter: one of the boats whalers carried. There are a few people on board, maybe three or four, and one is waving. I scan the horizon again and then look back.

But that's odd... now it's gone again. Perhaps it was moving faster than I thought, or maybe there's a strong current just offshore.

As if designed to drag me back to reality, here is an olive-skinned woman approaching me. I suppose she wants me to take a picture of her or something. I thought everyone did "selfies" with a phone these days but perhaps – happily – she's not in that unfortunate league. But now I see and hear that she's very bedraggled, and she's crying.

Oh Christ, why me? It's probably some stupid scam or other to get some money. But no, she explains in faltering English, between big sobs, that she's lost her daughter. She's either a superb actor or is in real trouble.

What the hell, I know I have to help. She really is frantic. The little girl was with her but must have wandered off, right on the edge of the water. The woman is frightened because the child can't swim.

I start walking quickly and shouting, I don't know the child's name so I'm just calling, "Hey, Hey, where are you?" I start feeling the same panic evident in the mother's voice.

I've been shouting and walking about for ten minutes or so, looking hard for signs – any more footprints – but it's a waste of time. There's absolutely nothing.

Dead End Tales

I turn around. Bloody hell, this is ridiculous! The woman is nowhere to be seen.

This walk of mine has just moved up a gear; slipped into the bizarre.

I'm not a little shaken, spooked even, and in need of a cup of tea. Or maybe something a bit stronger.

I start to slog up the shingle, breathing heavily. It's hard going. I'm a bit tired and sweating after these odd things happening – or maybe, not happening. At the head of the beach there's a paved path through the trees. An antiquated sign indicates "Refreshments". I follow it and, ah yes, good, here's a nice-looking little cafe in a ramshackle building. Time to sit and have a drink, and perhaps treat myself to a snack.

It's quite old-fashioned, with trinkets everywhere, and lots of crocheted place mats. On the wall I can see an old, framed newspaper, the paper yellowing, with those characteristic brown spots. The headline carries a story of a shipwreck almost a hundred years ago to the day.

I've ordered a hot, sweet tea, and while I sit and hug the cup I study the story to see if there's a drowned or lost child. No mention of that, just thirteen people saved from a Spanish vessel, the Sighing Lady. I check with the cafe owner; no, he's not heard of anything out of the ordinary, no ghostly appearances on the beach, no apparitions of women crying, just the usual visitors. He starts to complain about the way the local council isn't doing enough to promote tourism in the area. Nodding sagely, I hurriedly drink my tea and leave.

I'm working from home today, in my little study overlooking the garden.

It's a week since I returned and first recounted my strange experiences walking on that lonely beach. The memory has already started to change into another rum old story to tell. My wife listens patiently as I run through some of the peculiar details again. I can sense that I only have half her attention. She has things to do; she kisses me on the cheek and bustles downstairs.

The computer irritatingly shows I have dozens of emails to attend to, so I drag myself back to it. I push the button on the radio; a little bit of music will make things more bearable.

Ten o'clock. A jingle is followed by the national news: the European situation, a new viral epidemic, the Middle East, the price of oil…

I am not really concentrating, but then I hear the name of the area where I was walking.

"…when the engines failed last night. The Señora Suspirando, registered in Spain, ran aground on a sandbar in heavy seas and is believed to be breaking up. Rescue attempts by RAF helicopters have been hampered by the strong winds but thirteen people have been air-lifted to safety. A lifeboat was launched from the ship but was overcome by the swell, and four people, including a woman and child, are missing."

The window is open, and a breeze sends a deep shiver down my spine. There's an odd aroma.

The doorbell rings and I hear my wife answer. I can just hear her speaking over the sound of a Spanish lady, who is crying.

~ ~ ~

First published in The Lock Keeper's Cottage: Short Stories of Mystery, Ghosts and Horror *by Henry Curry*

Granny Grace

Wendy Fletcher

Granny Grace had always been my favourite Grandmother. Granny Margaret was okay in her own way but not half as much fun. It was always Granny Grace who had the wicked twinkle in her eye. She made us all feel that we were her favourite grandchild, especially me, of course.

Being the only girl gave me an advantage over my three brothers. Being the smallest increased my advantage. My parents always thought having me baptised in her honour, Grace Eliza, was the deal breaker but no, I walked off with that favourite title entirely down to my dark curls.

Her two sons were both pale and gangly specimens and they had their father's sandy hair. In turn, they both married girls with a hint of auburn and finally along came the ginger, sandy, freckled weaklings that claimed to be my brothers and cousins. The rest is history.

So, you can see why Granny Grace's heart melted when several years later I was delivered into her arms for the first time, a plump, gurgling, mirror image of her younger self. Anyway, that's how it all started. Long before I learned how to manipulate the situation.

Dead End Tales

I was the child who could always get the last slice of cake with just a winning smile while the boys were told it was half an hour to teatime and to get their dirty hands washed before they even thought about coming into the kitchen.

I could get a second chance in our games, another throw of the dice, or another flick of the tiddlywink with hardly a wheedling sound. My bond with Granny Grace grew as I grew. I took every opportunity to spend my time in her company.

So, it was hardly surprising to anyone present when I said how much I loved Granny Grace's pretty emerald ring, and she sighed wistfully, replying, 'Well, I won't live forever, dear. Then it will be yours,' totally bypassing both my mother and my aunt.

The other thing I loved about Granny Grace was her house. Granny Margaret had travelled a lot and lived in foreign countries and had good stories to tell, but her house was modern and smelled of spray polish – shoes off at the door.

No such rules at Granny Grace's house. Straight in from the muddy garden and up the stairs, usually accompanied by at least two hairy dogs and often a few other kids who had come to play when they heard we were visiting.

Here we could be riotous rather than righteous. As we grew up, time with Granny Grace became limited to school holidays and uni vacations. We were a mixed bunch, lively and animated as we started to make forays into the world.

Sometimes the discussions lasted all night, with Granny Grace keeping up the pace, providing snacks and cans of beer as we lounged on comfy sofas and expounded the social merits of communal living or the spiritual advantages of island isolation.

I was still in high school at that time, but my predicted A-levels results were good enough to assure me a place studying criminal psychology, my chosen subject. I had always been fascinated by how the mind works.

What turned some to crime while others endured worse experiences without once straying from the straight and narrow path? With a future doctor of medicine and a future doctor of theology in our group, we explored all possibilities.

At that time, we had no inkling of how those theories would be tested when the effects of crime came calling closer to home. We were in our twenties then, and Granny Grace had sadly passed away.

It was soon after her death that her empty house was burgled. We were, of course, upset by both the event and the timing. The police were more baffled by the strange behaviour of the culprit.

Locally, this particular miscreant was quite famous, or should that be infamous? With a string of offences on his record, he had bragged about how easy it was to sell on the spoils of crime.

But this time was different. The police had arrived to find fingerprints not wiped, a dropped glove near to the back door, and a canvas holdall stuffed with money and jewellery in the hall.

In a ransacked drawer in the bedroom, a box had been prised open. In it lay the beautiful emerald ring that Granny Grace had promised me all those years ago. Revealed but untouched.

'He must have been disturbed.' The police asserted, but not convincingly. They had only been alerted when the passing postman had happened to notice a curtain moving next to an open window.

No-one claimed to have been on the lane outside or to have had any cause for suspicion in the preceding days. No-one reported that anything amiss had been noticed that week.

There had been no unusual activities noted, no strangers lurking in nearby gardens, no unexplained noises in the night, no way of determining exactly when the crime had even occurred.

Enquiries at nearby houses brought no new information and eventually it all came to rest on the forensic team, those telling fingerprints on the window frame, and fibres collected.

The matches were good. There was enough evidence now to proceed; a conviction was pretty much in the bag. Just the sort of tidy end that everyone liked.

The offender was on first name terms with local officers. It was a short drive to his house. They didn't even have to look up his address.

Expecting total denial, they had the forensic report ready to wave at him. It would be a victory of sorts to see the arrogant teenager squirm.

The case was solved. What they wanted to know was what had disturbed him. That was the mystery. His silence came as a complete surprise.

It seemed unlikely that anyone would have been passing the isolated house, but they stuck with the theory as they had no better one.

This time there were no stories filtering through the gossip-vine. No-one had heard any rumours, any protests of innocence, nor even any boasting.

Silence was maintained right up to the day of the court case and the chamber was unusually quiet as we filed in.

My brothers now held their respective degrees, and I had my head full of theories and a hypothesis for every occasion.

Yet none of us were able to fathom why this usually vocal teenager had said nothing – not a single word.

Our only source of information was our long-standing family solicitor and even he was more than a little puzzled.

He could only say that the defence team were voicing concern about the mental state of their client.

Apparently, it was as if he had suddenly lost the will, or the ability, to speak out.

Then he was in the hushed room, eyes downcast – not the rebellious bravado I had expected.

I had wondered if this was a tactic to gain the sympathy of the court.

But now I just saw a frightened boy with hands clenched to his sides.

Everyone was seated. The moment of truth could not be delayed any longer.

Tension could be breathed in the room as the heavy doors closed.

The only sound was the shuffling of papers on a desk.

Would he offer any defence or explanation? It looked unlikely.

Could he not speak because of his trembling jaw?

Dead End Tales

Surely all this couldn't be an elaborate act?
An expectant silence hung in the room.
Time seemed to have been suspended.
Would he take this opportunity?
Would we ever know?
Eyes stared ahead.
He mouthed.
'Ghost.'

Jane Potugee

Shadrack Bones and the Case of the Humane Rat Trap

Philip Cumberland

It had been a quiet time for Shadrack Bones and, although the postman delivered letters most days, new cases had been thin on the ground recently.

Amy was working on combustion research for a French car manufacturer. She was assisting her old professor three days a week in a college laboratory nearby. Her income helped them keep their head above water while Shadrack waited for paying work.

Today was one of the days Amy was at home. Bones scooped the letters up from the mat as soon as they landed, sorting them as he walked quickly to his study. He placed them in piles of perceived importance on his desk and then set to with the letter opener, a fierce-looking dagger he had taken off an attacker in Paris.

He had misjudged the letter from Lord Archimedes Pendle Grope in terms of importance, and it was one of the last to be opened. He unfolded the stiff, heavy notepaper and read quickly.

"We have an enquiry from Lord Pendle Grope, Amy," he exclaimed.

"The Humane Rat Trap man?"

"The very same."

"They die laughing. Who would think that rats laugh, but they do?"

"What on earth do rats laugh at?"

"That is a good question. We will have to ask his lordship. What does he want?"

"He has not said, just asked me to call on him at his house in Buckden, Huntingdonshire, as a matter of some urgency and importance. I will telegraph him to say we will be with him as soon as we can and see what trains are available."

At midday, they arrived at the imposing large red brick and stone house of Lord Archimedes Pendle Grope. Bones put its date at late seventeenth century.

The horse and trap from the station drove in through the large stone-pillared gateway along the sweeping gravelled drive, before dropping them by the stone steps that led to a large studded dark oak door set in a stone arch. The iron knocker was in the shape of a dragon; Bones lifted its tail. When it dropped, the noise was colossal.

The door was opened by a large middle-aged man of military bearing, wearing a tailcoat, waistcoat, and matching pinstripe trousers. Bones introduced himself, and his wife as Doctor Wilkins.

Passing the butler his card, he stated he was there to see Lord Pendle Grope. The butler asked them to take a seat in the entrance hall while he took Bones' card on a silver tray to his employer.

A few minutes later he was back to show Bones and Wilkins to the oak-panelled library on the first floor.

Pendle Grope was a small, plump, elderly man with unruly long white hair and a florid complexion. He wore gold-rimmed spectacles.

Bones introduced himself and Dr Wilkins. Pendle Grope shook hands with them both, inviting them to sit down. When the three of them were comfortable in the deep leather armchairs, Bones asked his Lordship to outline his problem. Sensing Pendle Grope's hesitation, he explained proudly that not only was Dr Wilkins an eminent scientist, engineer and doctor but also his wife and partner.

"*The* Doctor A Wilkins?"

"I know of no other," replied Amy.

"I read your paper on the combustion process in petrol engines. When it said Dr A Wilkins, I thought it was a man."

Bones spoke, "Rest assured, sir, I would have noticed by now if she were."

Amy blushed. "He makes frequent inspections to make sure."

"Right! To business." said Pendle Grope. "My invention, the Humane Rat Trap, works by subjecting the rodent entering the trap to a fatal dose of a form of Nitrous Oxide."

"Laughing gas," said Amy.

"Quite. It is presented in the form of a solid rectangular block, inert until it is activated by urine. Rats urinate frequently, nearly continually in fact. The block of chemicals has an attractive sugary smell. When the rat enters the trap, it urinates on the bait to mark it as its own. As it does so, the gas is released in copious and lethal quantities. Once the gas is released, the trap is automatically sealed containing the gas within, so it presents no danger to other living creatures. When it is safe to do so, the trap is taken outside, the gas safely discharged into the atmosphere and the dead rat removed. The trap is then ready for re-baiting and further use."

"I see." Said Bones

"The reason I have called you in is that half a ton of the bait has been stolen from my factory in Ely and held for ransom. If I don't hand over ten thousand pounds by Friday, the bait will be dumped in the sewers of Cambridge University."

"Is the bait activated by any form of urine?"

"Yes, Doctor Wilkins, only a small amount would be needed to trigger the process of release."

"And the gas released would backfill through the colleges?"

"It would, and with lethal consequences."

"What I suggest," continued Pendle Grope, "Is we travel to Ely to my factory. I have my personal train in steam at the station. It can get us there within the hour. My chauffeur will drive us to the station in my car. Were cars a more reliable means of transport, we could drive directly to Ely."

In fairly short order Pendle Grope, Amy and Bones were driven to Buckden railway station. The three were soon seated in a well-appointed carriage of a train that consisted only of that carriage and the green tank engine, its locomotive. Bones marvelled at the wealth that could afford to keep not only a locomotive in steam at all hours but the means of securing rapid progress through a rail network belonging to several different railway companies. Peddle Grope's factory had its own siding, complete with a platform.

Bones spent the journey deep in thought while Amy chatted to their employer. Pendle Grope was flattered by Amy's attention and unaware that she was carefully gathering more information from him in the course of their conversation. Before reaching Ely, Bones had stirred from his reverie to ask Pendle Grope if he had argued with anyone recently, whether he had dismissed anyone from his employment, or if anyone had left on bad terms.

When he replied that he could think of none, Bones changed tack, asking if anyone had recently joined the company and left shortly afterwards. Pendle Grope could only think of one man, Addison, but said he would check with his foreman to be sure. Addison, the man in question, was a shipping clerk and had been with the company for just three months before leaving. Significantly, he lived in a village near Cambridge served by the railway.

They alighted from the train, entering the factory by a back door. This was Pendle Grope's normal means of entry and raised no concerns with his workforce. The noise of the approaching train would have given some warning.

Bones and Amy were taken on a tour of the factory, starting from where raw materials were unloaded from railway wagons, together with coal for steam engines which powered the factory's machinery. The works were divided into two sections, one part where the traps themselves were manufactured and assembled, the other the chemical factory where the bait was produced. The bait was sold in packs for replenishing the traps and also supplied packaged with new traps.

"In what form was the bait stolen, sir?" asked Bones.

"It was in four wooden crates and loaded onto a train for Cambridge. In the same truck were a number of complete traps, over three hundred."

"Were there any other crates of bait on that train?"

"Yes, another eight."

"When was the theft discovered?"

"The following day. The train had been left in a siding at Cambridge. When the customer came to collect the consignment, some of the crates were found to have been forced open and the contents had disappeared."

"The bait within the crates, was it in bags or boxes?"

"It was in jute sacks."

"Were any vehicles seen in the vicinity of the wagon?"

"Only a coal cart. It came into the siding empty and left empty. The paperwork for the collection of his coal wasn't ready."

"I see," said Bones, "and has the coal merchant been back since?"

"He came back yesterday, unloaded his coal from the truck, weighed and bagged it before loading it onto the cart."

"Where did this take place?" asked Bones excitedly.

"Further down the track in the same siding."

"Do we have a name for this coal merchant? And when the theft was discovered, were other trucks nearby searched?"

"By Jove, Bones, do you think the coal merchant moved the bait into his coal truck overnight?"

"We have to consider that possibility. Is the coal truck still here?"

Within a few minutes, the three of them were back on the train, steaming at full speed for Cambridge. Pendle Grope had telegrams sent ahead to the station master, asking the questions Bones had put to him. If the coal truck was still there, he was to ensure that it wasn't moved.

The line from Ely to Cambridge is short and direct. Pendle Grope's train was routed to a nearby siding. The engine driver produced a set of steps and helped his passengers down onto the pebbly ballast of the siding.

Bones and Wilkins inspected Pendle Grope's wagon first. Bones searched the floor of the wagon minutely, using his magnifying glass, and he spotted something of interest in one corner.

"Look at this, Wilkins," he exclaimed.

"It looks like a brass button, Bones."

"Exactly. Did you notice the coal dust near the boxes of bait?"

"Yes, I was about to mention it."

Pendle Grope had left Bones and Wilkins when they clambered into his wagon. He was back now with the name of the coal merchant: Albert Standing of Newmarket Road, Cambridge.

Bones and Wilkins then moved to the coal truck. There was still a surprising amount of coal remaining inside. They didn't immediately notice a large pile of coal in one corner.

When the truck was jolted by a shunting locomotive being coupled to a truck further along in the siding, the pile of coal started to collapse. As it did so the corpse underneath was gradually uncovered, Pendle Grope looked into the truck as the corpse's face emerged.

"By Jove, I know that man. It's Addison!"

Bones climbed into the truck, then carefully lifted the lumps of coal away from the body. Addison's coat had small brass buttons; one of the lower ones was missing. Wilkins took the button found in Pendle

Grope's wagon from her bag and passed it to Bones. It was a perfect match.

"We will have to fetch the police," said Bones. "It seems he was involved, or at least present during the robbery."

Bones was anxious to get away, impatient to visit the coal merchant. After what seemed an inordinate length of time, the police arrived. Bones chafed until Wilkins, Pendle Grope and he were able to give their statements and leave.

Pendle Grope had a cab waiting for them at the station and with great haste, they made for the coal merchants in Newmarket Road.

Within twenty minutes they were at the doors of Albert Standing and Sons Coal and Coke Merchants, but the establishment looked closed, and as if had been for some time.

Bones paced up and down on the pavement outside, deep in thought, smoking his pipe while Pendle Grope, Dr Wilkins and the Hansom cab waited, the horse snorting impatiently. At last, Bones snapped his fingers.

"Cabbie, I want you to drive slowly around the colleges. We are looking for coal cellar entrances close to sewer manholes."

The light was fading. Two possible candidates fitted the criteria. The first, St Peter's, was situated within the city centre. The other, Aldernol College, had its coal cellar next to its cast-iron manhole cover in a quiet side street that was overlooked by the tall, windowless stone walls of an adjacent college. The street, Aldernol Terrace, led down towards the river Cam.

Bones and Wilkins alighted from the carriage, and Bones asked the Cabbie to wait around the corner. Pendle Grope remained in the cab, out of sight.

Wilkins and Bones linked arms and strolled casually down the cobbled terrace towards the river. They were both looking for a likely hiding place for the coal cart and also somewhere to hide unseen to observe the coal cellar. At the end of the terrace, the couple turned around to walk back. A few lumps of coal were of interest, near the doors of a windowless stone building nearer the river. The snort of a horse from within also caused Bone to raise an eyebrow. It was now early Thursday evening.

Bones and Wilkins walked back along Aldernol Terrace. Tinkerland Road, the street at right angles at its end, had a building with a loading door high in the wall. A wooden beam above it protruded into the street; Bones pointed it out to Wilkins.

"I think we could watch the coal cellar from there, Amy."

An hour later, two shabbily dressed workmen made their way along Tinkerland Road. One was considerably shorter than the other. The pair looked around the outside of the building and spotted a door at a corner. The door was tried and found to be locked One of the workmen pulled tools from his pocket and within a minute the door swung open inwards.

"Have you got your electric torch, Amy?"

Although Amy hadn't brought her handbag, the workman's leather tool bag contained all she needed. Amy passed the torch to Bones; he switched it on and shone it around the building. It seemed to be a store – a greengrocer's by the look of the open hessian sacks standing around the walls, containing potatoes and carrots. There was a wooden staircase in the corner.

As the light faded from the torch, Wilkins said, "It needs winding, Shadrack."

As Bones turned the key on the torch, the light returned, and a brown rat ran across the floor, exiting through a hole in the brickwork.

"They obviously haven't got one of Pendle Gropes traps, Amy."

"No, it appears not."

Amy, who was shaking with fright, ran to Bones for a reassuring hug. "I hate rats, Shadrack. They scare me."

"I don't care much for them either. Can you climb upstairs and keep watch, Amy?"

Bones led the way upstairs, holding Amy's torch to light the way. A gap in the boards of the door allowed a view down the street and of the coal cellar with its manhole. The wooden floor was strewn with straw. Sealed sacks stood against the walls. Bones pulled his revolver from his pocket and made sure it was loaded.

"Amy, can you keep watch? I don't expect much to happen yet. My guess is they will try to move the bait into the manhole once it gets darker but will have some means to prevent it from being released. If the ransom isn't paid, they will have a way of dropping it into the sewer. If you see any activity, shout down to me."

Amy shone the torch down the stairway until Bones was safely down; she had found a garden fork in a corner of the loft and had this ready to beat off any inquisitive rats.

Bones waited uneasily by the door, with more than one pair of red eyes visible in the gloom. Now and again, a rodent would race across the floor, squeaking as it did so. One rat ran across Bones' foot. A well-placed kick sent it flying into the wall with a squeal of pain.

It was a long wait before Wilkins alerted Bones to activity in the street below.

Bones opened the door and edged around the corner of the building. The coal cart was parked beside the manhole and coal cellar. The manhole cover had been removed. Two men were struggling to lift a narrow wooden drum off the cart. Several more drums stood on the back of the cart amongst sacks of coal.

Bones carefully edged his way along the wall lining the street, keeping to the unlit shadows. The two men were visible in the light of the street's solitary gaslight.

When he was within range, Bones lifted his revolver, telling the men to raise their hands. They obeyed.

Bones made them move away from the cart and stand by the wall, but he hadn't spotted the third man who struck him from behind with a club. As Bones fell, he fired the revolver. The frightened horse galloped away down the street. Sacks of coal and a wooden drum fell off the cart as it turned the corner.

Amy was waiting in the road as the horse galloped towards her. In an act of unbelievable bravery, she managed to stop the horse in its tracks.

The three criminals were racing towards the cart. After just a moment's hesitation, she leapt onto the cart, flicked the whip, and the horse moved off with the ruffians in breathless pursuit.

Bones, recovering from the club's blow, stood shakily, found his police whistle and blew on it with all his might.

He felt a spot of rain. There was a broken drum near the manhole with squares of bait near to it. Could rainwater release the gas? With difficulty, Bones managed to replace the heavy iron cover. He stood the drum upright and replaced what he could of the bait inside. The other drum was undamaged.

Two constables ran around the corner and asked Bones what was going on. He explained the situation to them as best he could and asked them to collect the bait and keep it dry. Before they could question his authority, he retrieved his revolver and set off down the street, hoping that Wilkins would be safe. He had no clue as to which direction Wilkins would take. Hopefully, she would make for the city centre. He turned a corner.

There, leaning against a wall, was a bicycle. Bones leapt on it and pedalled off, hopefully in the right direction. He was despairing of finding Wilkins, when he heard the clatter of hooves in a nearby street.

Rounding the corner, he saw Amy was in trouble. The fittest of the three men had managed to get onto the coal cart and was locked in a fierce struggle for the reins. The other two men were walking towards the cart, one holding his side as if he had a stitch, the other was limping. Both were breathless.

The ruffian fighting with Amy managed to push her off the cart and geed up the horse. Bones fired his revolver and, to the dismay of the man with the reins, the horse bolted again.

Amy managed to get to her feet and seemed none the worse for wear. Bones handed her his revolver and told her to cover the other two criminals as he pedaled off again as fast as he could after the cart and its galloping horse.

He caught up with the cart in King's Parade as the horse was slowing, obviously tiring. The cart's driver was too preoccupied to notice his approach. Bones grabbed hold of the moving cart and pulled himself on, leaving the cycle to carry on. The driver was distracted by the appearance of the bicycle overtaking them as Bones smashed a large piece of coal into the side of his head. The second, better-placed blow knocked him unconscious.

Bones was slowing the cart when the police arrived. They had already relieved Amy of her prisoners and now took charge of Bones' captive, who was still out cold.

All of Pendle Grope's bait was successfully recovered. The three miscreants were charged with murder, together with theft, extortion, and blackmail.

Pendle Grope's gratitude took the form of a very large cheque, rewarding the couple's efforts and putting them onto a sound financial footing.

Murder It Ain't!

Sandra Hughes

'Murder she wrote,' often on TV,
but never written by me.
But on waking this morn,
with many a yawn,
that word in my head,
I thought of this instead.

'I could murder a cup of tea.'
A phrase sometimes used, but not by me.
'You're murdering that song lass.'
Another I bypass.

'She'll murder him when he gets home,
drunk as a skunk,' his friends moan.
'The new babysitter lets kids get away
with murder.' A bit extreme, that one, I'd say.

And did you know,
you could have murderous feelings?
Feeling extremely angry, furious, irate, seething…
Murderous desire really exists.
Numerous words, you should see the list…

Dead End Tales

Eager for bloodshed,
bloodthirst, bloody-minded,
cutthroat,
homicidal,
sanguinary,
sanguineous,
slaughterous…
It's certainly extending my vocabulary,
and a dictionary find.

This homework has my knowledge extended.
Not sure this was what was intended.
There is also, 'murdered by words,'
had you heard?
Comebacks, counter-arguments, puns.
You know… the ones you think of much later,
or next day,
but at the time you did not say.

I have to confess, murder books generally
I do not read.
Although Midsomer Murders and Father Brown
I concede
I have watched on TV.
Lighthearted, their murders you see.
Not real, make believe, just a show.
Sorry, scriptwriters, to deliver that blow.

There are many words used to describe murder.
Not really something I wish to explore further.
However, if I want my writing to expand,
I should make the effort; learn the 'brand.'

Dead End Tales

Murder, manslaughter, homicide…
My brain's shutting down, I'm not getting on-side.

Although there are many employed in this field,
seeking out criminals,
hoping crime scenes, will yield
the very clues needed to solve the case.
Much more intense these days,
avoiding wrong arrests and the guilty still free.
Murder really isn't for me.

Jane Pobgee

Jane Pobgee

Worse Than Death?

Hilary Woodjetts

So, there I am, lying on the hospital bed with my head in a funny piece of headgear, and I'm thinking, why am I looking down at my body? It's not two minutes ago that I was on top of the ladder, trying to get out of a sticky situation.

If her husband hadn't come home unexpectedly, I wouldn't have had to make the lover's traditional hasty exit. I had quickly left via the window, after we heard his car pulling up and realised we would be caught in flagrante delicto if I didn't shift myself fairly soon.

However, in preparing my method of escape, I had erected a ladder underneath their bedroom window. It was the old wooden type and not in the best of conditions, and the dust that came off it wasn't dust at all, but frass from the nibbling of greedy woodworms.

(My recommendation is, if caught in a similar situation, go for a metal ladder. As long as it isn't showing marked and abundant signs of rust, it should be up to the job of supporting your weight as you climb out. Unlike the wooden one I chose.)

After the top rung disintegrated, my descent was impeded by several more rotten ones as I slipped inexorably towards the ground, loosening my grip in shock as I went. I think I screamed, and I know I didn't put all my hastily jettisoned clothes back on.

And, basically, I don't remember anything more than that. Not being picked up, not being transferred into an ambulance, not being carefully looked after en route to hospital, nor anything else save the whooshing sound I felt rather than heard before my vertiginous ceiling location.

I watched as the doctors and nurses desperately tried to revive me. I felt a momentary tickling sensation in my soul, I suppose, but no driving urge or call to get back into my body, twitching under the paddles of the defibrillator. Oh dear.

Then the realisation hit me. I'm a ghost, a spirit, an other-worldly being. The capacity for mischief is endless... all those people who have wronged me, called me names, cheated me out of my small chance of wealth. And eternity to wreak havoc.

Starting with my scuzzbag of a wife – she who ran off with my best friend. And him, of course. Let's see... could I begin with them and deflate the tyres on his BMW? Yes, I could, with a little bit of effort.

Job done! The crunch of the metalwork against the tree and the tears of my erstwhile beloved as she stands at the side of the wreckage are most satisfying. She has to run as the car combusts, her lover satisfactorily fried.

I have only to think it, and I am at the location where I want to be, with her I want to see most: my beautiful lover, with the face and body of an angel, married to an alcoholic bastard.

Of course, if he hadn't been one such, she wouldn't be in a foetal position on the hall floor as he punches her. It's easy to make a sound upstairs… 'Have you got somebody else as well, you bitch?'

That's right, me boyo. Up you come. He takes the stairs two at a time in his haste to see who else might be there. The surprise on his face as he meets an invisible fist is farcical.

He tumbles backwards, lying at an unnatural angle at the foot of the stairs. The shock stops her wailing momentarily as she scrambles to dial 999, saying she doesn't know whether she wants police or an ambulance.

She'll be all right. I'll keep a watching brief on her as she settles into a better life. She'll have a sizeable sum from my will, so she can leave behind all vestiges of this life.

Of course, I hadn't expected to shuffle off this mortal coil so early in my life. But my father died intestate, and my mother visibly aged, sorting out the mess. So, on my 30th birthday…

Scuzzbag and I had no children. She didn't want them and made sure I wouldn't sire any before we married – tying the knot twice over, I suppose you could say. What a blessed relief.

The things you remember when you have no time left to enjoy them… camping with my brother in Switzerland when our parents finally let us go off on holiday alone. And the girls…

And the fights when we both went after the same girl. Scuzzbag was one of them – he had a narrow escape there. I think he realised it, too, and was very thankful.

Even on our wedding day he stage-whispered, 'Are you sure you want to go through with this?' Maybe that's one of the best man's duties – averting impending doom or divorce.

Unfortunately, she heard him. So did her father. Fisticuffs were averted by the vicar stepping in and hauling us off to the vestry for a few straight words about impediments.

Because of that, I hadn't seen my brother in years. I thought I'd look in on him. Um, yes. Well, he's obviously very happy with his wife, Ilona. Very!

Discretion being the better part of valour, I scoot along to my nephew's bedroom. He should be asleep… no, he's looking at nude women with his headphones on.

I used to listen to my Walkman under the blankets, reading a book by torchlight when I was his age. Then came computers. I never looked back.

'Halllooooooo, Michael,' I say to him in my best sepulchral voice. 'Shouldn't you be in bed now? And what are you watching, you naughty, naughty boy?'

Alarmed, eyes wide with fear, he dives into bed, nearly knocking over his chair as he goes. 'W-w- where are you? Who are you? Go away!'

'I'm the ghost in your machine,' I whisper. 'I see everything you see, and what I have just seen makes my eyeballs pop out.

'Where's the excitement of discovery going to be when you finally grow up and find a nice girl to settle down with?'

'I am doing it as part of my biology homework,' he whimpers. 'The study of the human body. It's all good.'

'The only human body you need to study at your age is your own,' I roar. The poor kid wilts.

I haven't yet got to grips with how ghosts manipulate electricity and the special effects department. But I'm learning.

So, I make the screen images disappear like TV screens used to, down to a dot, then phhht.

I leave too, giving my best ghostly laugh as Michael cowers, pulling the blankets over his head.

I decide, after a couple of days, to see how my beautiful lover is getting along.

I can't immediately locate her. Whizzing through the house, I begin to feel rising panic.

Perhaps she's done something really stupid. After all, she's lost both husband and lover.

That's enough to send anybody over the edge. Oh, hell, I hope not!

I quickly locate her upstairs, in front of the suite of wardrobes.

She's grimly sorting through her late (but not lamented) husband's clothing.

Tailored suits, expensive shirts, silk ties, underwear and casual gear.

All unceremoniously dumped in a big black plastic bag.

She's crying and sits on the double bed.

My photo is open on her mobile.

And then, she begins to laugh.

'Goodbye, you two. Good riddance!'

'Darling, are you there?'

Basso profundo voice?

What the…??

Ohhhh!

The Old House

Sandra Hughes

The house knew who it liked, loved. Those who appreciated living there. It knew who used and abused it. Those who added utilitarian rooms, allowing more folk to live there. Those who brought love into the house, and those who caused upset, discord and unhappiness. It watched, waited and acted.

The scarf she wanted to wear was not where it should be, where she had left it. Was it worth looking in other places? Was it going to be in a place where someone else thought a scarf should be? Would it be in a strange or amusing place?

Good job she wasn't in a hurry and had many other scarves to choose from. It was just that she planned her outfits in advance of outings, and that one went perfectly with the rest of her clothes. Maybe she could change her mind about the whole outfit.

That was a bit too far for her mentally, even emotionally. And look at how much time she'd been thinking about it. She smiled to herself and picked an alternative choice of scarf from the well-stocked scarf rack in her wardrobe. Perhaps it looked okay, she decided.

Thankfully, after many years in the same house, she was reassured that other family members would understand the reference to the 'missing scarf,' when she related it to them later over dinner. At least it was something very small and, to many, insignificant. It was interesting.

Others would imagine it had fallen off the rack, and was caught up amongst her many shoes at the bottom of her wardrobe. Someone else might suggest she had lost it last time she wore it; it was safe in a handbag. They knew better.

Other times, the loss was more important: a document required for an application; a much-loved ring; a vase for the unexpected huge bouquet that had been delivered. Amusingly, none of the children growing up had ever used it as an excuse for lost homework.

There were, of course, instances of footsteps heard overhead when everyone was accounted for downstairs, TVs coming on in the middle of the night, music heard from the radio when no one had switched it on, lights that turned themselves on. No-one minded.

Also, there were the many red admiral butterflies that appeared in the house, in any one of its rooms, at unusual times – any time of the year. Current family members welcomed the sight of them, seeing them as a comforting, spiritual sign.

Googling the butterflies, she found words that made her smile. 'They can signify things which are hidden and not as they appear.' Many things in her life had turned out not as they appeared. Mainly her ex-husband. Nothing like he appeared.

But it turned out she had been protected. The one who made everyone else walk on eggshells eventually left, with no way of returning. The house did not belong to him, and his disrespect lost him access to it forever.

In fact, he had abused the house and those within its walls to the extent that his ejection was final – from the house and from the country. The loss and humiliation would have hurt him and his pride greatly.

Younger generations were drafted in to take over. The house breathed a sigh of relief. Gradually, it was looked after, renovated, rejuvenated, restored. Young voices rang out; young feet running up and down the stairs. They loved it.

The century-old straw was removed from the loft, and mice ejected. Modern cladding replaced the straw. Central heating was updated, meaning no one was ever cold, or ill again with pneumonia due to the damp and cold.

The old front doorway was uncovered, and the original coloured glass appreciated and noted. Interested in the history of the house, they unearthed the original deeds and parchments. Retrieved, these were hidden surreptitiously from the ex.

Neighbours, who previously avoided the house with its unpleasant owner, took an interest, helping to dispose of the hated bottle bar. They offered advice, assistance, friendship, and many tales of the house and previous occupants.

The house listened, agreed and settled contentedly. It was going to be a happier home, and this family deserved it. Youngsters enjoyed their rooms once again. It was a house meant for young people.

Those had been words spoken to a woman who thought this would be a new start for her and her children. She had believed it to be her dream home – a white cottage.

But, it turned out, that imposter could turn it instead into a nightmare and, at times, an unsafe place for all of them. Sometimes, the house gave them respite – rooms to escape.

This had been so different from the quiet harmony in which she sought to bring up her children. The house tried to help. It loved children and enjoyed them being there.

The woman and the house were determined. The family have fond memories of fun and laughter at holidays and celebrations with grandparents, friends and family, visiting for Christmases, parties, barbeques…

The miserable one had been turfed out of his den occasionally to participate, forced to engage and, dare they say, enjoy himself? In spite of himself, he did. Sometimes.

Mostly though, he remained locked in his cave, with his addictions and bad moods. Only the house saw and knew. Others avoided him, stayed away, leaving him hidden.

An invasion of mice went down in history by forcing action from the man of the house when one landed in the waste basket next to him.

But, by now, inertia and lack of interest in his home had led to neglect and deterioration. Windows threatening to fall out became a safety issue.

Dead End Tales

The roof had leaked for many years. The children's rooms, with umbrellas and buckets, had no heat. The woman had no room of her own.

She was working full-time, worn out with no money for treats or outings. Her friends and family were cut off. But her love continued.

The house saw and heard all of it. The house felt it all. Still the house continued to offer its comfort and sanctuary.

The house saw all his secrets: his lies and deceit, and the money he had stolen from the house and the woman.

The house had tried to protect the woman and the teenagers as they grew into adults. Their partners had helped decorate.

They did their best to maintain the house and keep it in good repair. They showed concern in practical ways.

The house appreciated their attention and loving care. Butterflies began to appear regularly in the house, whatever the season.

The dogs watched over certain areas and corners of the house. They weren't barking. What were they seeing?

Her son-in law still regales them with his memories of their family in this amazing old house.

Their wedding reception, their children growing up, halloween pumpkins carved. Memories still live in its walls.

Memories of his son, parents, brother, uncle… all still watching over those under its roof.

He and his have done so much to benefit and preserve this family home.

He, his wife, his family are deserving of the house and its protection.

The house knows it well, and she knows it only too well.

All the friends and neighbours of the house know it too.

Do friends and family guess the secret of the house?
Why is this such a sanctuary for the family?
What is the presence that haunts every room?
What friendly spirit hovers, watching over all?
What makes this a survivors' home?
Happiness embedded in its walls.
What magic is circulating
under its roof?
The answer?
Love.

When to Keep Your Mouth Shut

Cathy Cade

There's murder in my heart.

I grind my teeth (silently) and rest my chin on my hands, with fingers (unobtrusively) over my ears, while I try to read through this job description.

But I can't concentrate. The slurp, munch, chomp, grumph, gets through. Although the hands-over-ears help me feel slightly less on edge.

I once read a newspaper article about women who feel like murdering their husbands over the dinner table. Until then, I didn't realise the problem was me – not the masticator.

Misophonia is a sensitivity to certain sounds such as chewing, pen tapping, sniffling, or throat clearing. Its main symptom is distress when hearing the sound that triggers the reaction, causing a fight-or-flight response.

I'd always put it down to bad manners on the part of the muncher. I mean, is it so hard to keep one's mouth shut when eating? Must the baked beans be sucked in? What is difficult about opening the mouth to put in the fork and closing it again before masticating? How can anyone slurp pastry?

Don't get me wrong, my stepfather is a lovely man.

Dead End Tales

Bill welcomed us into their home when I turned up on the doorstep with daughter and dog in tow after finally leaving my control freak of a husband. I'd been trying to move without wincing after Liam's last outburst when I realised that Lucy was avoiding him too. Until then she'd always run to him when he came home, for a hug and a tickle.

She may have picked up negative vibes from me or from the dog, but Liam was already looking at me askance after Lucy's reaction, so I knew the blame would fall on me. How long would it be before he turned on Lucy, too? I packed what we could carry, clipped on Buster's lead and we caught a bus to the station. (The cab wouldn't take dogs.)

Don't be fooled by Buster's name. Liam had hopes of a Staffordshire Bull Terrier bolstering his coveted tough-guy image, but you'll get an idea of how fierce Buster is when I tell you that little Lucy held the other end of that lead all the way to the bus stop.

I'd phoned Mum while we were on the train, and Bill was there to pick us up from the station.

Bill and Mum have been married almost three years now, and I've never seen her so happy, even when Dad was alive – although those last months must have been gruelling, so they don't count. Dad would have known he was ill when he gave me away at my wedding seven years ago, but he said nothing to any of us until later that year, when the effects of his chemo were too obvious to hide.

When we first arrived here, Lucy shied away from Bill, as she now did from Liam. Bill didn't push it, and now she comes to him for cuddles and calls him 'Gammy' (which he is rather, with his arthritic knee). Buster curls up at his feet while we watch TV in the evenings. Dogs and small children seem to have an instinct that adults lose somewhere in their teens.

Bill is reading his newspaper while I read through the job application in front of me. The silence is broken only by the gentle background whoosh of the dishwasher... and the slurping across the table.

I wanted to say, "Would you like a straw with that?" but the last time I'd said it out loud, I'd ended up with bruised ribs. Not that I thought Bill would react like Liam. Bill would be apologetic and a little bit hurt, and I'd never forgive myself for hurting this gentle bear of a man.

With Liam, I learned early on to keep my sparky comments to myself. He always seemed to take them personally, even if they weren't about him. ("Always got to be the clever one, haven't you, Bella?" Nobody else called me Bella – not since school, anyway.)

Through the years that followed the bruised ribs, I'd come to feel genuinely murderous sharing that table. I'd considered crushed pills in his dinner, rat poison, dodgy mushrooms... I'd even researched online. Apparently, poison is women's weapon of choice, but mushrooms are something of a cliché, murder-wise, crushed glass doesn't actually work, and anything accessible is detectable post mortem.

As things got worse, I was almost ready to risk detection. But I had Lucy to think of.

"I'm hungry, Mummy. Can I have some more breakfast?"

I glance at the clock. "It's a long walk, Lucy. We don't want to be late for school."

"I can drop you on my way to work if you like, Izzy. I've a job out that way today." Bill keeps busy in retirement with odd jobs and a bit of gardening.

"Can I have choco pops this time?" She hitches up onto the chair next to Bill and he pours a measure of cereal into the bowl I've not yet cleared away after her cinnamon bites.

He pours the milk. "Is that enough?"

She grins at him. "Thank you, Gammy," and shovels in a mouthful.

I can't stop myself... "Please shut your mouth when you're eating, Lucy."

"Why?"

"Because I don't want to see what's in it, and I don't want to hear you chewing."

But to be honest, the noises don't stand out when other people and sounds are going on around us. It's that slurping into the silence that gets to me. Perhaps there's hope for me after all and I'm not as unbalanced as a true dyed-in-blood misophonic.

I'd expected Liam to come after me, but he's no braver than Buster when faced with male opposition. While Bill is getting on a bit, he's a big guy, and his work keeps him fit.

And Liam isn't muscular. He tries, but he doesn't have the staying power. His gym attendance is sporadic and his musculature is reminiscent of Popeye before the spinach. In fact, if I joined the local gym and took up a self-defence class...

But first, I need a decent job. Gyms don't come cheap.

I don't have much of a CV. Liam was against me going back to work after Lucy was born; he liked that I had to ask for money to go shopping. I suppose I ought to talk to someone about getting money out of him for Lucy, but right now I don't want to stir up the dung heap. I'm just relieved he hasn't turned up on Mum's doorstep; he must, surely, realise where I am.

My cookery diploma, coupled with college's first aid training, quickly landed me a part-time job in the kitchen of a local private school. They'll pay a little extra if I'm one of the school's required (and currently under strength) team of First Aiders, so tomorrow I must take in my refresher certificate (obtained in my own time, of course).

Work is close enough for me to drop Lucy off at school and pick her up after I've finished, which is almost worth more than the pittance they pay me. But at least now there's something on my CV and money to spend on clothes in the charity shops. I wanted to contribute to the housekeeping, but Mum won't hear of it.

Today, I have the day off in lieu of working next Saturday for the school's Open Day. Buster and I enjoyed our walk in the sunshine, instead of me getting up at silly o'clock to walk him before breakfast. We return through the side gate, as I do every morning, and I bend to unclip his lead before bolting the gate shut.

In the garden, Buster growls at the back door.

"What's the matter, boy? Smell a rat?"

I'm not far wrong. In the kitchen, Liam leans against the sink, arms folded, triumph in the beady rat-eyes I once read as darkly romantic.

Buster growls in the doorway. Liam takes an apple from the fruit bowl on the table and tosses it into the garden. The dim dog follows his Pavlovian instinct and chases after it. Liam closes the door and locks it, pocketing the key as he turns.

"Hello, Bella."

He moves to the hall door, and I edge in the other direction, keeping the table between us.

"What are you doing here?" Silly question. My voice wobbles treacherously.

"I've been here for a while, watching you." Over the weekend? Or longer? He will have called in sick at work. "You didn't think I'd let you get away with taking my daughter and my dog off me, did you?"

"You don't want either of them. You wouldn't know how to start looking after a six-year-old."

That isn't his point, though. It's me getting away with it that he can't allow.

Buster barks outside the back door. Liam closes the hall door and leans against it.

"I need to go and pick up Lucy from school."

"Not for three quarters of an hour. Plenty of time yet."

Time for what?

I slide a knife from the knife block behind me. I'm not much of a threat with a table separating us, nor even without it, come to that. But I feel a little bolder.

"I've applied for a court order. If you harm either of us…" Buster barks again, "…any of us, you'll be locked up."

His eyes harden, drilling into mine. Whatever he reads there seems to reassure him. How long has he been watching us? Does he know I haven't been to the police or seen a solicitor? Nonchalant, he leans on the table and takes another apple from the bowl.

"No, you didn't. They'd have been to see me."

He sneers and takes a bite from the apple, munching noisily while maintaining his sneer. It's a horrible sight.

"And it'll be too late by now. The bruises will have faded. They'll want to know why you left it so long."

He takes another ostentatious bite, reminding me that he still has a full set of teeth, since none of his have been knocked out by his nearest and dearest. It's a scornful, macho sort of bite, more than he can easily chew. Grinning and grinding, saliva dribbles from his mouth. His tongue comes out, and he slurps it back.

I cringe.

Buster barks. Liam chomps and I hurl the knife.

Like a fractious child.

I watch the blade turn in the air.

He flinches as the handle hits his chest and then throws his head back to laugh.

It takes a moment before I register the panic in his eyes and realise he has yet to let out that intake of breath. Drool and fragments of apple fall from his open mouth. Small fragments.

His face turns scarlet. His hand hits the table, then thumps his chest. The Heimlich manoeuvre.

Does it work self-administered? I hope not. I'm trying to recall what we covered in last weekend's refresher session.

He's making a strange noise now as he slips to the floor.

As I fumble in his pocket for the back door key, he grabs at my wrist, but I easily hold his arm away with my other hand. I let Buster in. He runs past the twitching body and under the table. I pick up the knife and return it to the knife block before going out to unbolt the side gate.

Back in the kitchen, I leave the back door unlocked, grab my handbag, and retrieve the dog lead.

"Here, boy."

He's at my feet already, tail wagging at the jangle of his lead.

I pull the front door closed and hear the lock click.

Lucy is pleased to see us at the school gates, soaking up the warmth of the afternoon sun.

"You brought Buster to meet me!"

"We've been in the park all afternoon. It's been so nice… I thought we could go back and have an ice cream."

"And I can play on the swings."

"As long as you don't need me to push you. You know Buster isn't allowed in the playground."

That should be long enough for Mum to get back from her "Knit and natter" meeting and call the police.

While we finish our ice creams, a police siren wails nearby. Lucy goes into the playground, leaving me to watch her from the bench, while Buster touches noses with passing dogs. Soon after, a neighbour joins me while her daughter runs in to the playground to greet Lucy.

"Izzy, what's going on at your place? A police car pulled into the road as we were leaving and two officers went into your mum's house."

"I don't know; I've been out all afternoon." I stand and beckon to Lucy. "We'd better get back and make sure Mum's okay."

Lucy doesn't want to leave now her friend's here, so the neighbour says she can drop her home later. It's an excuse to come and find out what's happened, but the scene will be easier without Lucy there. With luck, they'll have removed Liam by the time she gets home.

I'll tell them I wasn't there this afternoon when he must have let himself in.

Well, I wasn't, was I?

The girl in the café made a fuss of Buster – she'll remember us. I'll say we went straight from the park to pick up Lucy from school.

The girls run back to the playground and the neighbour wishes me luck.

"You know, I did wonder this afternoon why Buster was barking in the garden. It isn't like him to bark at nothing, is it?"

I open my mouth, but nothing comes out.

Jane Pobgee

The Secret of Ramshaw Rocks?

Valerie Fish

Jutting out of the Ramshaw Rocks, part of the Roaches in North Staffordshire, sits the Winking Man. As you drive past this colossal stone goliath, a trick of the light creates the illusion of a winking eye.

Local legend has it, women who are fortunate enough to witness this unusual phenomenon may soon hear the pitter-patter of little feet.

I like to believe that he's winking at couples driving by, on the way up for some shenanigans amongst the rocks.

But, many years ago, there's a possibility that a couple travelled that way with something truly horrific in mind…

It has been suggested that photographs taken of Ian Brady and Myra Hindley were shot up on those rocks.

If that were true, who took the photos?

And could it be possible that Keith Bennett, the only victim whose body was never recovered, lies somewhere up there?

Keith's poor mother went to her own grave not knowing what happened to her dear son. I doubt we will ever know now, the evil b****** never having revealed those facts.

If Keith Bennett is up there, that Winking Man would be instead shedding tears that the couple passed below him before ascending the rocks to commit their heinous deed.

Jane Pobgee

George's Bungalow

Sandy Snitch

My father built the bungalow, and for fifty years he lived here with my mother. I lived here until my marriage.

When he had accrued enough off-cuts of wood, he built the first conservatory. Wood was on ration like everything else in the early 1950s. Later my mother replaced it with a white metal and plastic one.

Dad grew azaleas and tulips to greet the spring for my mother, who rarely went into the conservatory. She had banned Dad from smoking in the house, banishing him and his tobacco to the conservatory. She said she was "being kippered" by the smoke. She was also "sick of his betting".

Dad was offered a job at the local betting shop where he spent his afternoons, always winning, and able to sort out his winnings more quickly than the aged computer.

He only spent two shillings (10p) on his bets, and never more than ten shillings (50p) in a day.

When Dad died, the bungalow became my mother's. She immediately had the conservatory demolished and replaced with a bigger one built from glass and metal, part of which is still here today.

When mother died suddenly, I inherited the bungalow and decided to keep it as a source of income in my retirement.

In the early 1960s we moved into the bungalow for five weeks. It was January 6th, the place was dripping wet from the plaster to the concrete floors, and some windows had no glass. I borrowed a toilet door from the old house, and it was our front door, held in place by a huge utility wardrobe and a pile of broken bricks.

My bed was made of feathers. It was always cold, as the single-bar electric fire hanging on the bed-head didn't give out much heat. I don't know how it didn't burn the bedding when it fell. It must have been luck that the plug fell out of its socket as I tried to move it over the heaped bedclothes, and the fire only scorched the bedding.

At least it was warm for a while!

We decided to let the bungalow.

A young couple moved in and furnished the conservatory as a play area for their two-year-old daughter who spent a great deal of time playing in there.

When the couple moved out about a year later, I received a phone call from the mother, asking if anyone had died in the bungalow. I told her of my father's death some years previously.

She told me that her daughter would not go closer to the TV corner than about two feet. She would just stand still and stare.

I told her she must have connected with my dad's spirit.

The little girl spent most of her days in the play area where she had an "imaginary friend" called GeeGee who she spoke with frequently. She said GeeGee told her stories and she laughed at them. She told him what she was drawing and painting and would stick her artwork on the windows and doors with Sellotape or glue. (Some of them were there until the conservatory was replaced.)

I believe without a doubt that the little girl had connected with my dad's spirit.

In fact, I often think I can smell cigarette smoke and flowers in that conservatory and remember how he would freeze while smoking out there, wearing a heavy coat, hat, scarf, two pairs of socks and one glove...

After all, he wouldn't want to burn the other one.

A Haunting Discovery

Cathy Cade

Since the day we moved in, I've told family and friends
of the ghost that is haunting our house.
How it turns off the lights and makes noises at night,
(though my husband said that was a mouse).

And it's true, over time,
as we've stripped and replastered,
repainted, replumbed and rewired,
that the humming has stopped
(though the scrabblings remain)
and the lighting stays on when required.

If I've dropped the odd paperclip, earring or screw,
even though I could hear where it fell,
I never could find it, however I searched.
Did our ghost spirit those off as well?

Hubby said I was nuts. I'd begun to believe him
when I heard the tapping that day
on our bedroom's high ceiling (tap-tap, pause, tap-tap)
as I folded our clean clothes away.

Dead End Tales

Out on the landing I eyed the loft hatch,
in a spirit of investigation.
Its ladder unfolded on pressing a switch:
another recent installation.

My body, though, trembled as I neared the top.
The tapping was nearer, though soft.
I gathered my courage and switched on my torch
as, shaking, I clambered aloft.

The torchlight threw shadows that shifted and leapt.
I wobbled and grabbed a roof beam.
The water-tank loomed. I directed the torch,
and something fell past in its gleam.

Then another, another, another drip flashed.
Water pooled as I watched each drop fall.
My ghost was a loose pipe (drip-drip, pause, drip-drip)
and not spectral tapping at all.

I searched out a spanner, no longer afraid,
and tightened each joint I could see.
For averting an imminent ceiling collapse
I gave thanks to the powers-that-be.

A voice said, "You're welcome!"
I jumped, dropped the torch,
and left it alight where it lay.
I've never set foot on the ladder since then,
from that day until this day.

Fugu

Ed Morris

Sandra was busy in the kitchen preparing the Friday evening meal for her MP husband. That she was looking forward to the long weekend after being on her own for two weeks was probably an understatement.

I hate it, she thought, *him being in London.* She glanced at the kitchen clock. *I hope he will be home soon.*

She had arranged for their friends to arrive at nine for drinks and a game of cards. The shrill sound of her phone made her drop the condiments and cutlery she had been carrying to the table. That damned phone!

"Yes?" she said. "Who is it?"

"It's Samuel. I'm at Euston Station. Should be home in about twenty minutes. See you soon, darling."

At six-thirty, Samuel arrived home. He let himself in. "I'm home, darling."

Sandra came into the hallway. She put her arms around him to give him a hug. He did not reciprocate. She stepped back a few paces and stared at him.

"Are you alright, darling? You look absolutely dreadful. Come, sit down before you fall down. Would you like a drink? Scotch?"

"Oh, for God's sake, woman, stop fussing. I feel fine."

"Well, you don't look fine to me."

"I'm going to take a shower and change these clothes, so give me a call when our evening meal is ready. By the way, what surprise are you conjuring up for me this evening?"

"Oh, it's a surprise you will die for. Though it would not be a surprise if I told you, would it? I definitely do not want to spoil the excitement. And with a good meal inside you," she said, mockingly, "you should have a good night's sleep.

At seven-thirty, she called up. "Dinner's ready."

He came downstairs carrying a large plastic bag. "Could you take my suit to the dry cleaners first thing tomorrow morning?"

"I suppose so." There was a look of anger on her face. "Is it necessary? You only just had that suit cleaned. And where is the rest of your dirty linen?"

"It's in the laundry basket," he snapped. "Look, Sandra, stop the questioning. Every time I come home from that place, you start. Just take the damned suit, for heaven's sake." He walked over to the record player and selected a record from his favourite composer.

She said, "I hope you are not putting on that boring Claude Debussy again." Samuel just grinned at her. They sat down to their evening meal and peace descended for a while.

"You seem a bit fractious this evening, Samuel. Is anything worrying you?"

He gave his wife a withering look. "Sandra, I have had a very trying time at Parliament for the last two weeks and what I do not need is you interrogating me, so just back off! Leave it, please."

"I've invited some of our friends around this evening. I thought you would find the company enjoyable." She spoke very quietly but, under her breath, was laughing with derision.

"I'm not in the mood," he said, seeing the disappointment on her face. "I'm sorry Sandra but–"

"Samuel!" Her voice rose in exasperation. "I have spent week after week after week on my own in this house, and I'm beginning to feel like a frustrated nun while you're away in that damn place in London. God only knows what you get up to."

"And what the hell is that supposed to mean?"

"You know what I mean – the perfume; lipstick smudged on your shirt collar where you have tried to erase it – the colour purple, if I'm not mistaken, is it not? And while we're having this discussion about your infidelity with your bit on the side, the sickening leftovers I find in your underwear and trouser pockets on laundry day make me physically sick at having to handle them. And your suit… well! It tells its own story. When you do come home, you're worn out with no energy left for me, to put it bluntly."

"Have you finished?" He paused for a few seconds. "When doing the laundry, you can always wear those marigold gloves I bought for your birthday."

Sandra bit her lip, as she was about to call him a bastard, but thought better of it.

When the atmosphere had calmed somewhat, she asked, "Did you enjoy the fish I cooked for you?"

"Yes," he said. "Fugu always tastes good the way you prepare and cook it. Who have you invited around this evening?"

Sandra had brightened at the prospect of an enjoyable evening with close friends and especially with Jane, who was like a kindred spirit. She could hardly contain herself.

"I've organised drinks and nibbles for the evening and have set the card table up in the snug. I thought, maybe a game of cards… or some other form of relaxing pastime." She gave a slight snigger.

"Who is coming around this evening?"

She gave a sigh. "Susan, Gregory, June, Paul, Jane."

There was a deep intake of breath when Jane's name was mentioned. "You know I don't like Jane, so why do you keep inviting her?"

"Jane is my closest friend," she said, "that's why. And the only reason you don't want her here is because she rejected your unwanted advances at the last party we attended, so get used to the situation. I hope your mood changes for the better. The last thing I want is this evening spoilt by you and your black moods." She walked into the kitchen and slammed the door.

Sandra had opened the card table and carried it into the warm, cosy snug. She loved the room for its rich décor. For her, it was a place of refuge and contemplation where she read her favourite books and magazines and could listen to her own music while her husband spent his time ensconced in his London flat.

Well, that is where he pretended to be; Sandra knew better. *He's probably with his femme fatale.*

While arranging seating for their guests, Sandra's thoughts drifted back to the time she met Samuel. Yes, he was tall, handsome, athletic, (especially in the bedroom) very attentive and romantic; he had swept her off her feet. They married; children came along. Life was good – that is, before he became an MP.

She caught a glimpse of herself in the mirror. *I must do something about my weight. Yes, that's what I will do – sign up for keep fit classes.*

Samuel had known her parents were wealthy. They had even bought them a house as a wedding present.

Divorce had been on her mind for some time because of his adultery, although she had to think of the children, who were at boarding school, and the effect it would have on them and her parents.

And, of course, if I divorced him, he could be entitled to a good payout. I cannot carry on with my life in this way. There must be another way out of this sham of a marriage.

Susan, Gregory, June, Paul, and Jane arrived at nine. Sandra relieved them of their coats and guided her friends into the snug. Susan made a point of telling Gregory, "This is what I'd love to have in our home. I fall in love with this room every time I see it."

"You will just have to keep falling in love with it, my dear. We cannot afford it. Now, if I had the salary and perks of an MP..."

"Gregory, shut up! You are embarrassing me."

"What card game are we playing this evening?" asked Paul.

"I thought three card brag to start with," said Sandra. "Then we can decide what to play later on." Everyone agreed. "Jane, can you help me with drinks?"

"I'll sort the drinks out," Samuel said.

"No, Jane and I can manage on our own quite well enough. You keep our guests entertained. You're quite experienced at that," said Sandra sarcastically.

"Sandra, you look a bit under the weather, darling," said Jane. "You're rather pale."

Tears welled in Sandra's eyes. "You know what the situation is."

Jane put her arms around her, stroked her hair and tenderly wiped away her tears. "You know you can't carry on like this. It's not fair the way he treats you."

"I know Jane. I've made my mind up. I will carry out what we talked about."

Just then, Samuel walked into the kitchen.

"Hello! What are you two girls whispering about?"

"Oh, just girly talk," said Jane. "Nothing to worry your little head about."

Everyone was now sitting around the card table to start their game of three card brag and gossip.

"Haven't seen you for ages, Samuel. Are you still working from your parliamentary office?" asked Paul.

"Yes, of course," Samuel replied. "Although there's talk of some departments relocating to Manchester. Levelling up, they call it."

"Wow! That will cramp your style a bit, won't it?"

Jane gave Paul a sharp dig in the ribs, followed by a black look.

"Hang on! That was painful, and it hurt."

"If you make another remark like that," whispered Jane, "I'll hit you where it really hurts."

Samuel was shaking with anger. "What the hell was that supposed to mean?"

Paul, taken aback by Samuel's aggressive reaction, blanched visibly. "I thought…" The veins on Samuel's neck stood out and his face seemed to bulge. "Steady, old chap. I was only making conversation and not alluding to anything in particular."

Their friends stared at Samuel, not believing what they had just witnessed, except for Sandra, who hummed a little tune to herself.

Samuel recovered his composure and apologised for his outburst, putting it down to the pressure of work and being absent from his lovely wife for too long. Sandra rolled her eyes. She knew what he was working at in London, and it wasn't pressure of work. The only hard work he knew was gratifying his lust and performing between the sheets with his intern.

The friends played a few hands of three card brag. Sandra checked the time on the new Versace watch she had found as she sorted his clothes for the wash while he showered. Jane saw the watch as Sandra exaggerated the act of looking to check the time and squealed, "When did Samuel give you that Versace watch?"

"I think he meant to give it to me this evening. It – er – fell onto the bedroom carpet as I was checking his dirty laundry. I'm so, so sorry if I spoilt your surprise, darling. I know how much you love to surprise me."

Samuel's face was bright red, and he was looking uncomfortable as he struggled to respond. Sandra smiled with deep satisfaction.

Gregory suggested, "Let's have a change and set up the Ouija board."

"What a brilliant idea, Gregory. Come on everyone. Help Gregory arrange the letters. Someone get a small glass from the cabinet."

"I'll sort out more drinks," said Samuel.

"No, you stay in the snug and help with the setting up. Dim the light to create an atmosphere. Come on, Jane. Give me a hand with the drinks."

"Sandra, darling, you really don't look well at all." Sandra burst into tears.

Jane put her arms around her. "Is he still messing with that intern?"

"I've just about had enough. I only stick with him for the sake of the children and my parents. They would be devastated if they knew what was going on. And if I divorce him, he is so devious, I could lose my children and end up with nothing."

Jane gently wiped away Sandra's tears. "Our plan is foolproof. No one could prove anything, and you'll be free. We'll do it tonight. Is everything prepared?"

Sandra showed Jane where she had stored the liquid and warned her to handle it carefully.

In the snug, there was a single light over the card table. The letters of the alphabet formed a circle, with the inverted glass in the centre. Sandra and Jane passed the drinks around.

"Yours is a whisky, darling. Your favourite malt I believe," said Jane to Samuel with a sickly smile.

They sat around the table enjoying their drinks, Samuel with perspiration forming on his face and shirt. Looking decidedly damp, his eyes focused over Sandra into the darkness of the room.

"Stop staring, Samuel," said Jane. "You're giving me the creeps."

The glass tumbler began to move as if pushed by an invisible hand, navigating from letter to letter. The friends stood, slowly backing away from the table. They could not see the object that was mesmerising Samuel, though: a long, slender, grey hand of a woman with broken fingernails. It was spelling Samuel's name and asking, "Why... why, Samuel? Why?"

Christina! Samuel's scream tore at his throat. His eyes bulged with terror.

"Dear God, what the hell is going on?" asked Gregory as he dived for the phone to call emergency services. Paul and June knelt to try to comfort Samuel, who was still clutching his throat with one hand while pointing the other alternately at Sandra and Jane.

The medics arrived and Samuel was rushed into hospital as he slipped in and out of consciousness. Sandra followed the ambulance in Jane's car to give them time to go over their story.

Samuel lived long enough to tell Sandra the affair with his secretary was over. He had finished with her that Friday morning. He did not elaborate on how he had terminated the sordid affair, only that he had lost his temper with her. Then Samuel breathed his last breath.

Or so Sandra thought.

After Sandra had left, Samuel opened his eyes and beckoned Dr. Vandra over to his bedside. With his last ounce of strength, he told the doctor he had been poisoned by his wife and her friend with the Fugu fish he had eaten for his meal that evening.

Before leaving the hospital, Sandra asked what the cause of her dear husband's death could have been.

"We are not sure, although it could be poison. Cyanide springs to mind. There will have to be a postmortem with the necessary authorities informed."

Jane drove Sandra back home from the hospital to await news from the laboratory. Dr. Vandra said he would contact her as soon as he received the results.

"What are we going to do, Jane? I'm terrified the police will find out what we have done."

"It was an accident and nothing more," said Jane. "They can't prove a thing, so calm down. You are free and now we can be together."

On arriving back home, they found Gregory on the phone to someone at the hospital. Her friends gathered around Sandra.

"We've had some... look! Sit down, I'll get you a drink," said Paul.

"I don't want to sit down! What did the hospital have to say?" she said.

"I'm afraid... Samuel passed away just after you left him."

"No – no! Samuel passed away while I was there with him."

"Not according to Dr. Vander. I've just been speaking to him. Samuel managed to say a few words before he died."

"W – what... what did Samuel say?" stuttered Jane.

"They wouldn't tell me," said Gregory.

He asked if they would all like a hot drink.

"Oh yes, please," everyone accepted.

He returned to the snug with a tray of steaming hot drinks accompanied by sandwiches and biscuits. The events of the night were barely touched upon as they sat talking, feeling uneasy with the situation.

Their talking was interrupted by a loud knocking at the door.

"Was that the door?" said Jane.

The knock was repeated, although heavier and more insistent this time, so much so that the banging made Paul jump and spill his hot drink into his lap. He looked at his watch.

"Who the hell is banging on the door at four in the morning?"

He made his way into the kitchen to dry himself down while Gregory went to see who it was at the door. As he opened it, a large foot appeared between the door and frame, and the door was forcefully pushed open by an extremely large policeman with another backing him up. Out of the shadows, another man appeared in plain clothes.

"Good morning, sir. I would like to speak with a Mrs Quinn and her friend, Jane – I believe that's her name? May we come in?"

"Look, what's this about?" enquired Gregory. "It's been a very distressing evening for Mrs Quinn and her friends with the sad loss of her husband this evening."

"That's why we are here, sir! I would like to speak with the two ladies. I am Detective Inspector Andrews. Once again, may we come in, sir?"

On hearing the commotion at the front door, Jane ran to the bathroom.

Gregory introduced the detective to Sandra.

"Good morning, Mrs Quinn. Where is your friend, Jane? We would like to speak to her too."

"Jane? In the bathroom, I think," said Sandra.

"Can I speak to you somewhere private?" the detective asked.

Sandra looked around at her friends for a moment, then said, "These are my closest friends, and we have no secrets."

"Mrs Quinn, we are here on a most serious matter and I would advise your friends it would be in their best interests to move to another part of the house."

Sandra's friends couldn't believe what was happening. They were intrigued and didn't want to leave.

They agreed to move to another room.

The detective directed one of the women in the group to ask Jane to join them in the snug.

"I'll see if she's okay to join you," said June.

The group went upstairs to one of the bedrooms, and June tapped on the bathroom door. There was no response. She tapped a bit harder and called to Jane. Still no response. There was no sound or movement from within the bathroom.

She shouted for Paul and Gregory to please come and help.

The commotion alerted the police downstairs, who rushed up to the bathroom. They too hammered on the door. No response was forthcoming.

"I'm sorry," the officer said. "We'll have to force the door."

He put his shoulder against it and with one solid push, it flew open. Immediately, he told June not to enter the bathroom.

Jane had hanged herself with a dressing gown cord. There was nothing they could do for her.

Due to the circumstances Detective Andrews called a halt to his proceedings and said he would call Sandra into headquarters in due course, as part of investigations: into her friend's tragic death, and into her husband.

Jane had scribbled a note for Sandra and signed it to absolve her from any part in the murder of Samuel. The note was to be passed on to the police. It would safeguard Samuel's life insurance for Sandra and the children.

Dead End Tales

The two women had been lovers for years.

Sandra married Samuel to satisfy her own wish for children and her parents' desperation for grandchildren. Jane and Sandra had been living a lie, but their love for each other was sacrosanct.

Samuel, suffering pressure from both the Parliamentary Standards Committee – because of his indiscretions – and his heated arguments with Christina, his lover, had shoved her in a moment of madness, causing her to stagger backwards. Her head hit the side of a table, causing a severe skull fracture from which she didn't recover.

Samuel was under investigation for her murder.

~ ~ ~

"Oh, what a tangled web we weave when first we practise to deceive." Sir Walter Scott.

Ghost Training

Stephen Oliver

Do you know what the worst thing about being a ghost is?

Boredom.

You can see, sometimes.

You can hear, occasionally.

But you can't taste or smell or touch.

And there's no real chance of actually doing anything.

I mean, we've all seen *Ghost*, where you can interact with material things if you get mad enough. It doesn't work that way. At least, not for me.

But then, I've always been mild-mannered, rarely getting angry about anything, and then never for long. And even less so now because I don't have any glands or anything.

And most people can't see you, either.

You'll learn all that, now you're here with me.

You're the first... person I've been able to talk to since... I died. You seem like a nice enough guy, level-headed and all that. What happened to you?

Me? Well, I've never been a sociable fellow, you know. All I ever wanted was to create my art and maybe sell enough to live comfortably. So, people never figured much in my life.

Oh, I was a ceramicist. I made ewers and platters and things. You know, pottery, as the philistines are wont to call it. If you look over in the corner, you'll see a couple of my pieces she hasn't sold or destroyed yet. They're in my signature yellow and blue.

You do? I thought no one had ever seen my work outside of the arts and crafts shows. That's where I met her.

I'd hired a stall at the Annual Artisans' Faire and was trying to interest people in my stuff. But you know how folks can be. If it doesn't match Aunt Mathilda's curtains or Granny's dinner service, they don't want to know. So I hadn't sold a thing all day. I was just about ready to admit defeat and close up when she wandered by, billing and cooing and telling me my big plate was exactly what she'd been searching for.

We got talking as she helped me pack up the rest and the next thing I knew, I'd invited her to come back to my place to see where I worked.

Once we got here, I showed her around. She was especially interested in the big kiln downstairs, where I fired all my stuff. After that, one thing led to another and, before I knew it, I was in love with her. I started to take her out and spend as much time as possible with her.

She said she knew people who'd be interested in my stuff, and she could sell them for me. I got my hopes up and let her take a few pieces. She came back with some money, and I was over the moon.

We were getting along quite well when she came in all excited one evening. Said she'd found a wealthy buyer.

She mixed us a cocktail to celebrate, using the bottle of rum she'd brought with her. Unfortunately, I didn't notice that she wasn't actually drinking with me until too late.

The next thing I knew, I was standing here in the corner looking down at my body lying on the sofa. I knew at once what had happened.

She'd poisoned me.

Things like that are kind of obvious on this side of the Veil.

It didn't take her long to get rid of my body. She dragged me down into the cellar, my head bumping on every step, and stuffed me into the kiln. My ashes are probably still in there.

That's where she's taking your body, too, you know?

Hey, come back! Where've you gone? I'm sorry! I didn't mean to upset you.

Oh, there you are. Where did you go?

Really? My skull and everything still inside? Wow!

Well, now I know why she wanted me. She wanted my kiln to destroy bodies. Like mine. And yours.

Quiet up here, now, isn't it?

By the way, how did she get to you?

Me? She promised you'd get to meet me? Why?

Why, that's very kind of you. I've never thought of myself as a genius, but if you think so.

Well, now you have met me, just not in the way you thought you would. You were the wealthy buyer, I suppose. What did you do?

Ah, software. Anything in particular?

Really? Even I've heard of that. Never used it, though. Never was much of a computer user, to be honest. I've always preferred to work with my hands.

So how did it go with you?

Marriage and everything? Oh, dearie me, she really got to you. She's very good at that, isn't she? Lonely men with little experience of real life. Me, the shy artisan. You, the awkward computer genius.

How much does she stand to gain if you had your own computer company?

Really? No wonder she went after you.

How did she kill you?

Well, at least she's consistent. Poison and then burn the bodies afterwards.

Sounds like she's a real black widow type. We're probably not her first murders, either. She seems to have her technique down too pat for that.

What are you doing at the window?

Oh, that's the policeman she talked to about my 'disappearance'.

She told him she was my agent. Said I'd been depressed because nobody bought anything, and she was worried I'd jumped off the bridge.

And my body less than twenty feet away.

Is that a search warrant he's waving in her face? She doesn't look very happy about it, does she?

Damn it! You've gone again.

What? They've found your body? Good for them. I suppose they'll eventually find and identify mine too. I was at the dentist's for a check-up about a year before I met her, so there'll be records for them to compare my skull with.

No, I don't think anyone's going to have to worry about her in the future, either.

Hmm, there's a black limousine pulled up outside and the driver's waving up at our window.

What do you mean, that's your ride?

What? Like a limo service into the afterlife? Who'd have thought of that?

Hey! Let go of my arm!

I didn't know I could do that. Do you mean I could have left months ago? I thought the ghosts of murder victims were condemned to haunt the spot where they were killed forever.

Are you sure?

Thank you very much, that's very kind of you. If it's somewhere we can both be creative for the rest of eternity, I'd love to ride with you.

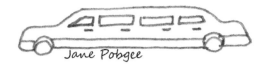

Jane Pobgee

Monkey Business

Wendy Fletcher

'So where are the Zaru brothers tonight?'

The man's bulk filled the doorway of the dingy cafe.

'Dunno,' came the mumbled reply from nearby tables as he scanned the shadows.

'Well, somebody better know.' He stepped forward. 'They better not have botched last night.'

A block away in an equally grimy basement the three brothers huddled over a rickety table.

'We're in here too deep.' There was more than a hint of fear in Mi Zaru's voice.

'Yeah, he'll have us seen to if we show up there and send someone to find us if we don't,' Mika Zaru nodded.

Ma Zaru said nothing.

At that moment the sirens sounded on the road outside. Too late to run, and nowhere to hide, the brothers could only stand in the gloom as the police broke down the door.

At the station they were held in separate rooms and questioned by different officers.

'We have witnesses that put you at the scene.'

'I never saw anything.' Mi Zaru insisted.

Next door his brother responded to the same statement, 'I never heard anything.'

In the third room, Ma Zaru said nothing.

'I think they're all too scared to let on to what they know.' The detective in charge shook his head. 'I'd bet my last pound that Joey Langham is behind this. This sorry bunch of chimps were probably only following instructions.'

'Well, that don't change the fact that a young girl's dead, Sir.' His colleague lowered his voice. 'And we are going to have to go and break the news to her grandfather. He's going to want some answers. Normally he takes the money to the bank himself every night when he closes up. Christ knows why he sent the girl last night, especially in that storm.'

Next morning saw the brothers released, pending further investigations.

'No-one's going to believe we saw nothing.' Mi Zaru's voice trembled.

'Or even heard anything, and the old grandfather's a real weirdo.' His brother shook his head. 'Word has it, he runs some kind of drug ring at the back of that pub.'

'That's all we need.' Mi Zaru's eyes were getting wider. 'A bloody gang of crack heads onto us.'

When the knock – well, more of a pounding really – shook the door, the brothers didn't know whether to hope it wasn't Grandad or hope it wasn't Joey Langham. It was too optimistic to think it might be a parcel from Amazon.

His eyes bored into them below whiskery brows.

'Word out there says you were in Mile Cross last night.' The measured voice was more frightening than if he had shouted.

'Yes, but I didn't see anything 'cus I was concentrating on taking pictures.' Even as he gulped the words, Mi Zaru knew how lame they sounded, but he dare not elaborate. If he mentioned they were recording the layout for Joey Langham, they'd be dead for sure.

'And I didn't hear a thing 'cus I had my headphones on.' Mika Zaru knew this was another pathetic pitch but what else could he come up with?

'And I suppose you were on the phone,' the old man turned his glare to Ma Zaru. 'Yeah, see, I have my contacts out there. You were on your phone, yet you couldn't call help for my Beryl.'

Ma Zaru shrunk even smaller than his five-foot frame.

'I don't think you bunch of primates did it, you haven't the brains between you, but I reckon you're all hiding something that I want to know.'

The hooded eyes scanned their faces. Each hoped that a twitching muscle wouldn't give them away.

It was another three weeks before the brothers disappeared.

'Just time for us to back off watching them.' The detective shook his head. 'Joey Langham is too smart a cookie to do anything while we had them under surveillance.'

'I'm not so sure about it being Joey Langham.' His colleague raised his eyebrows. 'I've been hearing funny stuff about that old grandfather. Never mind, as long as they've gone off our patch, it's three less scumbags to worry about.'

'Yeah, I might get a Saturday off at last. I was planning to take the kids into Norwich, perhaps let them loose for a run in Waterloo Park.'

'Never been there. Might join you for an hour.'

Saturday found the two men enjoying a stroll around the park, along the longest public herbaceous border in England, while the kids ran in and out of the pergolas, up and down the steps and walls, six acres of gardens to explore.

None of them looked up high enough to see the three brothers in their final resting place, coated in reconstituted stone.

Inspired by the sculpture by Alex Johannsen, of three wise monkeys who watch over Waterloo Park, Norwich, from their vantage point on top of the pavilion.

Based on Mizaru who sees no evil, Mikazaru who hears no evil, and Mazaru who speaks no evil, the sculpture has a modern twist of an added camera, headphones and telephone.

Murder They Wrote

Valerie Fish

The ladies of the Snottisham Cum Snitchly Creative Writing group were rather fond of murdering their husbands. The S & S Scribblers, they called themselves, as the whole thing would have been rather too much of a mouthful.

Every month, Enid would come back with a different tale.

'Gladys has done her Geoff in with a menorah. Poor fella didn't see it coming. All the ladies thought it was hilarious.'

George couldn't understand it; he didn't find it at all funny. He knew it was only a matter of time before he became the object of ridicule.

Enid had told him on more than one occasion that she was still debating on the weapon. When he jokingly asked her about motive, she'd replied with not even a hint of a smile that she had plenty of those.

Things had not been good between them for some time – ever since George retired, as a matter of fact. Enid had been looking forward to days out, more holidays, spending more time together. In reality, George was content to spend most of his time in his shed. What he did in there, she had no idea. He certainly didn't seem to be getting much gardening done.

So Enid, fed up with being left alone, joined her local u3a. It was one of the best things she'd ever done. First it was the walking group, then came local history, and finally where she really came into her own, creative writing. She'd always known there was a writer in her somewhere, just waiting for an opportunity to come out.

Everything was colour-coded on the calendar: second Thursday, for this; third Friday for that… George couldn't keep up with all, but no matter. As long as it didn't interfere with his goings on, which it didn't, he let her get on with it. At least while she was out, she couldn't be nagging him to death.

Thankfully, Enid would have no idea what he was really doing in that shed.

George was plotting a murder of his own. Except this one wasn't fictional…

Nothing was researched on the computer; George wasn't stupid. He knew all about deleted search history being traced. About the only time he did venture out of the house was to the library, where he'd research the old-fashioned way, looking up what he wanted in a real book.

He'd picked up some interesting ideas from what the other ladies had written. A few of them were not bad, he'd thought. Others he'd scoffed at, seeing massive holes in their stories. There was no way that it could ever happen in real life the way they had it mapped out. They obviously hadn't done their homework properly.

Dead End Tales

George was meticulous with his research. When it came to the actual deed, he would have only one chance of getting it right.

Unfortunately for George, he never had the chance to carry out his perfectly planned murder of the missus. Something happened he was totally unprepared for; something no one in the village could have envisaged, that shocked the S & S Scribblers to the core.

If George had his way, Enid would have already been gone. It should have been on the Tuesday, He'd have carried the whole thing off without a hitch, and be wallowing in the sympathy of the village, no doubt the Scribblers first in line with their sympathies and casseroles.

Enid put paid to that after a phone call from her ailing mother, resulting in a dash to her bedside an hour's drive away.

'I might as well stop the night, George, just to be sure she's okay. You know what Mum's like.'

George resisted the urge to comment.

It had to be Tuesday. The plan wouldn't work any other day. He reluctantly pencilled the following Tuesday into the calendar, mentally.

It all ended up happening on the Monday. One more day and things would have been so different...

George was in high spirits as he locked up the shed late that Monday evening (Enid was never allowed inside his domain) nervous and excited at the same time about what was to come the following day.

Standing at the kitchen window, drying the dishes, Enid saw – and heard – George come whistling down the garden path.

Enid didn't like George's whistling. She never had. In her mind, it had got louder and louder over the years. Many a time she wished she could shut George and his whistling up for good. She took the knife from the draining rack...

Was that her motive? Was it premeditated?

The jury believed so when they found her guilty of murder.

The S & S Scribblers never met again.

The very thought of murdering their spouses, albeit fictionally, was too much.

Of course, there were plenty of other things they could write about, but that wouldn't have been half as much fun, would it?

ABOUT THE AUTHORS

The Whittlesey Wordsmiths

We are a u3a (university of the 3rd age) creative writing group who meet monthly to share ideas and support each other. You can find your local UK u3a branch at https://www.u3a.org.uk/

Follow our blog at https://whittleseywordsmiths.com, or email us at… whittleseywordsmiths@gmail.com

Wendy Fletcher

Wendy is group leader of the Whittlesey Wordsmiths. Her first book, *The Railway Carriage Child* (available from Amazon) is a memoir of her childhood in the Cambridgeshire Fens, growing up in two Great Eastern Railway carriages. Wendy now gives talks about this to local groups.

She is currently working on a first novel as well as collecting memories and pictures to compile a social history of the small community in which she lived as a child. Her poetry has been published in *The Poet* (Christmas 2020) and you will find more poems and stories in anthologies from the Whittlesey Wordsmiths. Wendy is also editor of the magazine of the local u3a

Dead End Tales

and an occasional writer for *The Fens* magazine.

Find Wendy online at https://wendywordsmith.com/

Valerie Fish

Born and bred in London, Valerie now lives in the Fens with her husband of forty-five years. She has been writing on and off for most of her adult life. Now retired, she has more time to devote to her passion, with renewed enthusiasm since joining her local u3a creative writing group. She calls herself a 'Three in the morning writer', as it's often when tossing and turning in the early hours that inspiration comes.

As well as limericks, she enjoys writing flash fiction, particularly fifty- or one hundred-worders, regularly contributing to online challenges and having snippets published in the *Daily Mail*. Her book, *A Sexagenarian From Smithy Fen, and Other Limericks*, is now available from Amazon.

Find Valerie's blog online at
https://sexegenarianscribbler.wordpress.com/

Val Chapman

Having won a national essay competition at junior school in the North-East, Val decided to quit while she was ahead.

Life then got in the way and, with no prior experience, she thought she would pop along to her local u3a writing group on a whim and loved it.

It has taken Val sixty years to start this writing lark. It might take her another sixty to get the hang of it.

Aside from this new-found hobby, Val loves animals, cake, and her family. Sometimes in that order.

Stephen Oliver

Stephen was utterly sane until he was born to totally normal parents. Having been precipitated into this insane world without his permission, he decided that the only logical response was to become crazy.

He hid the craziness successfully while at school. However, when he started working, he came to believe he could speak to machines. The only possible solution was to train to be a software developer.

After more than three decades of this, he completely lost his mind and decided to become a writer. Over one and a quarter million words later, he's seen the publication of fifteen short stories, a dark urban fantasy anthology (*Paranormal City*), and a space opera novel (*Shuttlers*) in a single year. He's now madly working on another twenty-one books, some ready for publication, the rest still being written.

He says he'll only stop writing when they peel his cold, dead fingers off the keyboard. "Mind you," he quips, "knowing the kinds of stories I write, it'll be one of my own creations that does me in!"

His present philosophy is, "Only those crazy enough to believe they'll succeed, will!"

You can follow his lunatic rantings at
www.stephenoliver-author.com
and on Twitter @authorstepheno

Sandy Snitch

Sandy has always enjoyed writing poetry, and it was pointed out by her sons that they knew little about the extremely large family that she had known, and they had missed. So when a friend told her of the writing group she tagged along as a visitor. Having enjoyed what she heard, and the company, she joined the group.

Sandra Hughes

Writing has been an integral part of Sandra's life in her roles as teacher, project manager for *Mind* and as a preacher producing work magazines, sermons and reflections.

She has kept personal journals for over thirty years, finding it therapeutic and a useful outlet for the many thoughts and conversations rattling around in her head.

Having always enjoyed writing formal and informal letters, Sandra discovered a talent for writing poetry, useful in counselling and in life, writing poems for others at significant moments. Joining the writing group has been a most enjoyable and interesting experience, with homework prompts leading to short stories.

Sandra writes about her life with ME/CFS on her blog at https://wafflingwithme.wordpress.com

Dead End Tales

Rita P Skeats

Rita's working life began as a trainee nurse in the 1970s, working in hospitals in the East End of London. Later in her career, after having her two children, she went on to train as a midwife and worked at Queens Hospital in Essex until retiring a few years ago. Since retiring, Rita has moved from London to the Cambridgeshire Fens where she lives in blissful seclusion with her husband, son, many songbirds and a large garden.

Rita is a student with the Writers' Bureau studying a comprehensive writing course. Having joined her local u3a creative writing group, she benefits greatly from meeting like-minded people. In her spare time, she enjoys reading, creative writing, gardening, and being a slave to her daughter's cat, Raya. Once weekly, she and her husband attend an informal art group where she paints in watercolours and gossips over tea and cakes.

Find Rita's blog at https://ritasblog4.wordpress.com/

Philip Cumberland

Philip is possibly the oldest paperboy in Whittlesey and the Fens. In many ways that sums him up: he hasn't moved on much in many ways since his teens.

Born in 1951 in Paxton, he grew up in Huntingdon, spending his working life involved in the motor trade and engineering, the last thirty years of his working life running a small business.

For years, Philip has been fascinated with improving his art of writing but like many people didn't pursue his dream until later in life. A vivid imagination and the ability to inject humour into his writing are indicative of his youthful mind. More recently, he has been published in *Best of British* magazine, penned a variety of short stories, some of which are featured in this book, and published his debut novel, *Killing Time in Cambridge*, available from Amazon.

When he puts his pen down, Philip enjoys the Fens, music, reading, walking, cycling and being a general nuisance, according to his wife. Find Phil online at

https://fenlandphil.com/tag/fenland/

Jane Pobgee

Jane inherited her love of reading and storytelling from her mother, who would keep her daughters entertained for hours. Jane, in turn, made up stories for her own sons and later her granddaughters.

A talk by the Whittlesey Wordsmiths at the library encouraged her to go along to a meeting and have a go. In the intervening years, she has added drawing to her achievements, illustrating a number of the Wordsmiths' books.

Whilst they say everyone has a book in them, she feels she has a large collection of short stories. As her characters lead her stories wherever they want to go, she is looking forward to reading them.

Jan Cunningham

Jan is a lady of advanced years who always wanted to write fiction but never got around to it. Now with the help of the Whittlesey u3a writing group she is at last realising her dream.

Hilary Woodjetts

Hilary has had fourteen jobs in her working life, ranging from social work, guide at a Victorian working museum (where she learned to make plaster casts, dip candles, and black-lead cast iron fires), guide at a water and sewage treatment works (where she learned that some people really do want their false teeth back after they've been dropped down the loo), newsagent, bus driver, and – after a few other things as well – finally ended up as a University Chapel Verger. Not having had a career as such, Hilary says she has never been rich, but never been bored, either. She enjoys music (and was a pianist and church organist before her eyesight went wonky), reading, writing, but not 'rithmetic; travel, camping, and spending time with her long-suffering husband and their cat, who hitched a lift from France in the engine bay of their motorhome in 2008. (The cat, that is. Not the husband.)

Henry Curry

Henry retired in 2015 from a long career in telecoms with BT and Nokia. Born into a large family in Tottenham, North London, he has lived in Whittlesey since 1988 with his talented wife. In 1984, he gained a degree in science and technology from the Open University and followed this up with an uncompleted MSc in entomology. (He swears he will resume this, one day.)

In the mid-1990s, he and his wife were in a team of volunteers that set up and ran the National Dragonfly

Museum at Ashton Mill in Northamptonshire and, five years later, the Dragonfly Project at Wicken Fen in Cambridgeshire. He became secretary of the British Dragonfly Society in 2006 and served on their Board of Trustees for thirteen years.

Among his interests, Henry loves writing, classical music, computing, aeroplanes, buses, railways, photography, science, a bit of drawing, and natural history. For the last forty years or so, he has been madly passionate about insects, and dragonflies in particular.

Henry spends time studying, travelling, walking, trying to play golf, and writing. He began writing classes at City College in Peterborough in 2016 under the excellent tutorship of Tim Wilson and has been writing ever since. Since 2016, he has been on the committee of NAWG (the National Association of Writing Groups).

When not writing, Henry spends far too much time just staring at the wonders in his garden pond.

Gwen Bunting
Being an RAF service wife Gwen found herself in Peterborough. Making new friends has never been a problem.

She first started to write with Peterborough u3a Creative Writing. Sadly, the meetings were discontinued, and she found Whittlesey u3a, where she really enjoys the challenges.

Dead End Tales

Ed Morris

Ed began writing seriously while living in Australia. Returning to the UK in 1968, life got in the way and writing ceased. He returned to writing in 1989 with stories for children and had the privilege of reading them to children at their school.

Ed's main genres have been poetry and children's stories, although now, after joining the creative writing group at Whittlesey, he is keen to expand his horizons, Fugu being his first true effort.

Cathy Cade

Cathy is a former librarian who began writing in retirement. Most of the time she lives in the middle of fields near Whittlesey, occasionally relocating to a fringe of London's Epping Forest.

Cathy writes short stories with an occasional deviation into verse, mostly rhyming. Her stories and verses have appeared in both print and online anthologies and magazines, including *To Hull and Back Short Stories*, *Writer's Forum*, *People's Friend* and *Fractured Fiction Anthology II*.

Her books, A Year Before Christmas, Witch Way and other ambiguous stories, The Godmother, and Pond People, are available from Amazon and Smashwords.

Find Cathy online at www.cathy-cade.com

ACKNOWLEDGMENTS

Now all that's left to say is a big *Thank You* to all those who have made this book possible. That's all our Wordsmiths who have turned up, sometimes in appalling Fen weather, even on days when we had no nibbles to tempt them, and the heating was broken so we wrote with stiff fingers.

This is our first book in this genre so special thanks to Jane for her eerie illustrations and to Philip for our haunting cover picture.

Thanks to all those who have re-read, re-edited and rewritten their contributions and to Wendy and Hilary for their hours of proofreading.

Thanks again to group leader Wendy, who tries to keep everything together while working long hours and producing regular magazines for the u3a. And to Cathy who puts it all back together when it inevitably falls apart, as well as producing endless updated templates and fielding our million questions.

And, as always, thanks to our families and friends for their unfailing support and good humour, even when they were waiting to see if they would be the victim in our next misadventure.

Other Collections

from

The Whittlesey Wordsmsiths

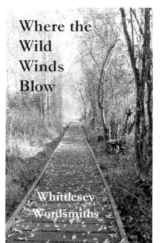

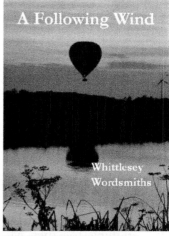

Available from
Amazon and
other outlets

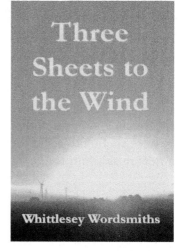

Festive Stocking-fillers

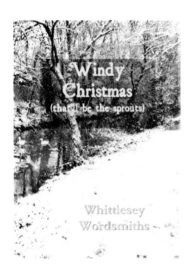

Other Books from Whittlesey's Wordsmiths

A memoir from Wendy

Phil's debut novel

Tessa's poems

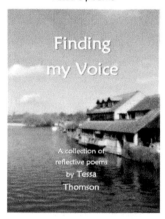

Val's limericks

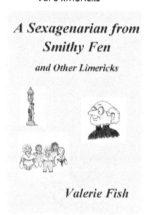

All available from Amazon

Dead End Tales

An eclectic collection of short stories
from Phil and friend

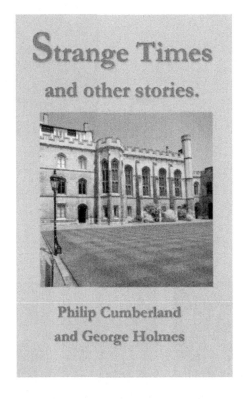

Available now from Amazon

Dead End Tales

From Cathy

Available from Amazon and Smashwords

~ ~ ~

From Stephen

Available from Amazon and Smashwords

Author Index

Dead End Tales

Dead End Tales

Printed in Great Britain
by Amazon

28429401R00121